The Three Graces

Also by Nan Deane Cano

Acts of Light: Martha Graham in the 21st Century. With John Deane. University Press Florida

The Three Graces

Nan Deane Cano

In Nan Cano's *The Three Graces*, cousins Marian, Norah, and Cara reunite at a crumbling family cottage. Each one's at a turning point brought on by grief and loss. This novel, vivid and complex, traces their transformations. As the characters travel to Costa Rica and Ireland, to California and New York, the story takes us into the worlds of professional dance, art history, the Magdalene laundries, and the terrible aftermath of 9/11. The perspective is at once global and deeply intimate. The writing compels us to care—these women and their lives matter.

Peggy Shumaker, Writer Laureate of Alaska

Published by Crab Creek Press

New York   Los Angeles

For Evan and Norah

Table of Contents

The Three Graces: Shelter Island

The Three Graces

Shelter Island

"When Sleeping Beauty wakes up, she is almost fifty years old." Maxine Kumin

1 The Goodbye Step

Marian rolled over in bed, waking slowly with the sense of a satisfying sleep drifting away. Eyes shut to keep the delicious rest in and around her, her right arm swung over the comforter, met by soft fur. Nelly. If Nelly knows I'm awake, it's all over, realized Marian, not for the first time. She played possum, pretending deep sleep and so fooled the patient labradoodle yet again.

Coffee aromas teased from downstairs. Paul rattled dishes, spoons. Marian heard his heels on the tile floor, a sign he was already off the exercise bike, showered, dressed and good to go. He was off for at least a week of trial work in San Francisco.

"Gotta get up, Nelly belly. Let's go see Paul!"

Nelly leapt off the bed joyfully, bounded down the stairs and plopped expectantly on the fourth step from the bottom, her good-bye step, hoping for Paul's hand to rough up her coat on his way out.

Marian waited, too, knowing Paul's routine as he checked his bags, files, cellphone, road snacks, one last look around. He would come into the front hall when all was in order.

"Here he comes, Nelly." Marian smiled at her husband, flirting through the dog. "Isn't he handsome?"

Paul shifted bags to kiss Marian and rumple Nelly up.

"Hey you two. Be good while I'm gone, ok? Take care of everything for me, Nell. You da dawg. OK. I'll call from the road after I get out of town. I decided to drive up the 5 and check on a few more pre-trial interviews I need to nail down. I'll be in Carmel by tomorrow and call you from the house. My cell's been weird so you might not get through. But the new computer lines should be running in the cottage so leave me e-mail, too, if you want. I guess I can try from the road, too, but connections are sketchy up there."

Friday, Marian would drive up to their Carmel cottage and work there while Paul went on to San Francisco. Nelly would roll on the beach and get totally, joyously, filthy.

"Okey dokey. I will find you. One more thing, though." She offered encouragement, arm around his neck.

"What? Gotta go. Oh—" and he kissed Marian on the cheek as she turned his way.

"It's a good case, Paul. I know you'll win. Don't worry about us. Be safe, ok? I love you."

And he was gone.

Marian likes arriving at her office at Immaculate
Heart College early enough to drink coffee looking
out at the fog gripping the Pacific coast of Malibu.
Swirls and rolls of grey cotton bales hunch over the
ocean, erasing the Channel Islands and their seals.
Seeing Catalina is an impossibility. She turns the
computer on, shuffles mail and faculty memos, ads,
and then sits, beginning to focus on Vermeer.

Shafts of light come from the left, just like the
Dutch morning casting thin blue-white veils over
the girl at the window. She is reading a letter. The
hint of a smile makes one think it is from a love far
away.

A gull flies by the office window, cruising,
coasting and then in a second thought flapping off
to the left. His grey and white body bullets by,
catching Marian's eye, moving her from the
Vermeer.

Thin sunlight struggles to pierce the gloom;
Marian looks up. Vermeer, had he been watching
Marian, would have known her. She was doing her
daily work with precision and craft. The light, sere
as it was, sanctifies her morning and encloses the
moment.

No moment would ever be just so again and it
was worth art and eye to seize it, even as it slipped

away. Fragments of this brief meditation curl into Marian's teaching consciousness as she turns from the pewter lit window back to the bright computer.

From the college homepage she clicks to Google and CNN for a news touch, clips of politics, Obama campaign workers, L.A. budgets, skipping across the screen. Local weather, California alerts for thickening fog. She clicks off the computer and walks across campus to meet her graduate students engaged in discerning the craft of Vermeer.

It isn't until quite late that night, lying on the couch, Nelly buried into her thigh, with Leno smirking through background chatter, that Marian sits up, startled.

She has not heard from Paul. No calls. No messages online or on the cell or house line. The late news interrupts Leno with a runner at the screen bottom of breaking news, and then she knows. Huge multi-car wreck on the 99 cutoff to Monterey.

She runs to the car and drives into the night.

2 Gone

Everyone in Madera had been really helpful. The small hospital was jammed, orderlies ran around with clipboards. Her orderly's clipboard was lime green, she remembered, with one piece of paper clipped to it, full of names. Paul's was fifth from the top. It was him all right. Blood all over his suit but his face remained unmarked, somehow.

> Dead.
> Gone away.
> Left the pavilion, as Monty Python said.
> Deceased.
> No more.

You go to school and study really hard. You go to a good college and find you love art. Its history, its stories, how its made, where it's made. You love singular and beautiful things with a passion. And you find a man. A great guy who winds into your heart, your body, your breath. You marry him and expect a family to follow someday. You get pregnant and love every fat minute of it until suddenly you are not pregnant any more and there is just blood. Blood like the blood in that morgue. Blood. So you go on and love and wait and pray to whatever childhood God is out there and there is only silence. No babies. But you love each other and work and go on and then one of you damn well dies. He was 55 and you are 52.

Is that all, really?

What Marian couldn't figure out for the life of her was what the hell he was doing in this one horse town. It was sort of on the route to Carmel, but still. Was this where a client lived? The last minute interview to nail down? She had only a vague idea, really, of the case at hand.

Paul would be sent to the mortuary in Westlake Village tomorrow, maybe. Signatures, certificates, paper, paper, paper , more blurred signatures. She took the bag they handed her, threw it in the car and turned around to drive home. To wait for Paul to come back.

It was just dawn.

The wails, the sobs didn't come until she walked in the front door and saw Nelly sitting on her goodbye step, panting, waiting for her.

She buried her face in the soft black fur and cried, holding on to Nelly, who nuzzled her in a worried fashion.

3 Pie

When your world is as small as mine, Marian thought, scrambling two eggs a few weeks later, it can disappear and no one would notice. There were no children to tend, no vast array of relatives, only the truly sad people in Paul's office and friends who sought her out, came from the college, brought food, flowers, said all the soft things one had ever said, and left. Gone with the wind. It was remarkably easy. Tidy.When she finally dragged herself into his downstairs study to pick through the briefcase she'd dumped that first night back, she realized how little she knew about Paul and his practice. Their time together, a sanctuary from the quotidian details, made them both feel separated from work and "out there." "Here" was calm, on its own rhythm. When one of them needed to rant or explode about work, well, they did. The other would commiserate and they'd try to put the issue aside.

The computer was still on. He had left it on when he left, and Marian couldn't bring herself to turn it off. The briefcase had briefs, handwritten notes, and files that went into a pile for Allison to figure out in the office. She'd know what to do with it all, contact clients, stop the work. Marian fingered his Cross pens, the wooden one she'd brought from England for him, the UCLA bookmarks and put them aside for herself.

The only true puzzles were in the cell phone with messages that made no sense to her and in one sealed envelope.

The college extended compassionate leave to Marian and for a few weeks she drifted, not doing much of anything. Hardly reading, ignoring house grime, turning away from the dying garden. Even the patient dog curled up quietly on days without sneakers and ball cap as signals for a long walk.

Today, though, one month after Paul's death, time stretched ahead like a desert road shining in a mirage to an unreadable end. Marian drove straight up 99 back to Madera. Madera was past the turn to Monterey where the crash happened, but information in the sealed envelope led her there.

She told no one where she was going the morning of Nov. 5. MapQuest rolled out her driving directions. Nelly was packed off for a three-night stay at the ranch she adored and Marian was on the road.

Pecan trees in perfect rows slipped by the highway. Grapes were finished and dry leaves hung off the vines, rustling. Corn still stood in dried out husks and fields of squash lent green and orange splashes. The road cut right through the valley. It was simple, clear, direct, as orderly as the passing orchards.

What was not clear or calm were the questions that pulled Marian back to this highway on a cold autumn morning. She'd made a list:

1. Who was Georgeanne Evans?
2. Why was her number on Paul's cell?
3. Why had Paul kept a letter from her in his briefcase in a sealed envelope?
4. What the bloody hell was going on?

Not exactly the way Nancy Drew would have phrased it, she reflected. But here she was tooling along in her roadster trying to solve a mystery. The engine began the hissing noise around 3 o'clock. Marian turned down the volume on "Hotel California" streaming from the radio and paid serious attention.

Shit.

Out in the tules with corn and grapes, not a town in sight and really scary noises.

"I'll take the next exit whatever it is and see what's what," Marian decided out loud. "I am not talking to myself; I am narrating events."

The car hissed even louder and faster stumbling along to an exit promising "Gas'" and "Food." A billboard advised one to "Bring your sin to the altar and drop it like it's hot." Further information could be had at seethelord.com

Janet's Diner, encrusted in rusty signs and a window full of miniatures of all kind stared Marian in the face. Only place open. "Take some time," one sign recommended. Marian entered the diner and settled into a red faux leather booth with kitty cats on the condiment holder, ordered a burger and lemonade and tried chatting up her waitress.

"I've got some engine trouble," she opened and Janet, her waitress/owner with her name smack in the middle of a flouncy hanky, agreed.

"Yup. Heard you comin' along."

"Is there a.."

"Not a real garage until you get to Madera, but Brian'll be along pretty soon. That's my son and he can check it out for you."

"Well, tha.."

"No problem, honey. You just set a bit. You look wiped."

I am not wiped, thought Marian. I am just fine.

The burger was good. Very, very, good. And the lemonade was fresh. Marian took out her MapQuest printout and an old fashioned map and unfolded it all across the yellow formica tabletop. She had 15 miles to go. It was 3:30. Factor in repairs and no telling what this night would bring.

Janet brought more lemonade without being asked.

"Hon, you want some pie? Lilly down the street makes 'em and they're real good. Pecan today."

"OK, sure. I never get to eat pecan at home because my husband hates nuts. Hated nuts."

And with that tense shift, tears found their way down her cheeks. She didn't make a sound.

Janet just stood for a minute and then offered softly "Men don't know what's good, honey. I'll just bring you a good -sized piece. Warm, too."

Well, good, Marian griped to herself. Here I am in Janet's Diner with blue kitty kats and I'm losing it. I have a map, a plan. I'm ok. Why the hell am I crying now, here?

Trying to stem the tears just made them increase. She felt embarrassed, exposed. At least the diner was empty except for one old guy nursing a cup of coffee from a white mug at the counter. Coffee, no caramel macchiato in this town.

Janet and the pecan pie arrived and the motherly looking waitress asked, "Hon you want to be alone or could you use some company. Business is slow today."

Marian sort of whispered, "Why not. Have a seat."

Thirty minutes later, Janet cogitated over the accident, the mysterious letter, Marian's fears—it all got spilt on the yellow formica to this stranger at exit 45.

Janet was ready. "Well, here's what I think. You got a shitty deal here and you're trying to figure out more than a letter, seems to me. I'm not saying your husband was fooling around, no disrespect intended there, but he was for sure doing something he either didn't **want you** to know about, or just maybe thought you didn't **need t**o know about. That could be a good thing when you come to think about it. Totally. And here's Brian now. You have some more pie and he'll check out the engine, 'kay? "

Janet smiled, patted Marian on the shoulder, which launched more tears, now of gratitude, and she did what Janet said. She ate more pie.

It was 5 o'clock when Marian drove up to the Madera address she had researched, pursued but now dreaded finding. She smiled thinking about the kindness of strangers, fortified by the simple gesture implicit in pecan pie, a good listener, and new alternator bearings.

4 Hope

Madera is far from Los Angeles, about 240 miles, and the light from the orchards, the rustle of corn husks with wind pushing through rows of gold slowed everything down to a more sensible level. Here Cesar Chavez stood his ground on grape strikes for farm workers in the 60's, small businesses tended to agriculture, a modest mall enticed shoppers.

Maybe Georgeanne Evans would be as simple as her town. There was the house: 33 Davison Avenue. The tiny white frame house stood primly on a small, clean yard. Two wicker chairs sat on the narrow porch, competing with four pots of cheery red geraniums in moist, clay pots. They'd just been watered. An American flag flew from a clamp on the left side of the porch and the front door had a poster for Obama—the one with his face looking

young and serious with colors varying across the picture and one word at the bottom: HOPE.
Marian sat in her car for about twenty minutes, watching. People came and went quickly. It was all very businesslike and those going in seemed to know each other. All had Obama badges or gear on. After a while, Marian decided to go in herself.

The door opened at her touch and a harried woman with short blond hair gestured her in with nods and a hand gesturing into the house as she kept talking into her cell.

"Just get us the numbers in 15 minutes. We are ready to go and these last minute delays drive me up the wall. I know, I know, just get the friggin numbers on my computer NOW." The blond disappeared into the crowded living room. The cell rang again.

"Right. Right. Yes. OK. I'll get the new script in 10 minutes, print it out and get everyone up to speed. Ted's our data manager for this session and he's already here. Later."

The woman turned to Marian with half a glance and called over her disappearing shoulder,

"Hey. Is this your first time here?"

"Umm, yes."

"OK, well you have a cell, right?"

"Umm, yes."

"So I'll be gong over today's script as soon as county s ends it to me. Pretty sure we'll be doing Nevada today."

"Actually, I ..."

"Don't worry—grab a soda or a water and say hello to everyone."

Marian interjected "Is Georgeanne around?"

"Yeah, but she is still trying to get this morning's numbers in and we're way behind. Oh, Jake! I need you NOW....." And she was gone.

Marian walked through the living room, dining room, kitchen, all full of people with cell phones and sheets of names and phone numbers. Most had Obama buttons on or shirts that said "Yes we can!" Or "All fired up and ready to go." Clearly, Marian had wandered into an Obama phone bank event with volunteers working for GOTV. Get out the Vote, the posters exclaimed.

Anonymous, unnoticed, receiving smiles, Marian wandered a bit, breathing it all in.

So Georgeanne's a Democrat, thank God. One check in her favor. Campaign literature and clutter filled tables, chips and donuts filled baskets on counters, and the conversations were humming with intensity. Marian decided to stay incognito a little longer, and just watch, see what happened.

When the blonde called everyone to order with a "People! People! Let's hit it here." Marian looked up to listen, her eyes grazing the group. An attractive slender woman about 35 walked in, a grin lighting up her brown-skinned face and announced, hand out, "Hi, I'm Georgeanne. Nice to see some new faces today. We sure can use the help. One more voice on those phones is great. For the next 3 hours I belong to Barack," the grin widened, "but maybe we can chat along the way. Please help yourself to food and let me know if you are confused."

Confused didn't cover it. Marian smiled numbly and picked up a phone list, ostensibly ready to GOTV. Coke and crackers in hand, she drifted along the fringes of the room. It was spare, but comfortable with a chintz covered sofa, low lamps, and photos scattered on tabletops and walls. This was an African-American family with humble roots, roots noted with pride. In one picture, a tall man stood on the edge of a field, hat in hand, grinning and waving. In another, three older women sat on a porch glider, faces turned expectantly toward the camera. It looked like one of them had just shared a joke. Photos of babies, school pictures, teams, and then Marian's eyes froze. Paul looked back at her. He was wearing his summer khaki slacks and the linen navy blue blazer she got him for his birthday a few years ago. The blazer was in his closet, right now. At home. He was standing in front of some official looking building—maybe a courthouse somewhere.

What the hell was her husband doing in this cheap frame? Maybe there's a pony in here, somewhere, Marian hoped.

Time must have passed, but Marian couldn't swear to it. Georgeanne was back.

"Thanks for hanging out so long. All the questions have gotten deeper than I'd planned for, but it's all for the good, and it's been fun, too. But how can I help you?"

Marian found her voice, which she thought had floated away.

"I'm Paul's wife. He died last month."

Georgeanne said nothing. Sat a moment.

"You need a glass of wine."

5 Secrets

Marian sipped the dark merlot while the house emptied.

Georgeanne sat next to her on the couch and not looking at Marian, began her story.

"It was in 2002. My brother was arrested for drugs and all he did was move in the house and close the door. My family does not do drugs in any way. Just don't. And Larry was stuck in the middle that night. He'd come by to drop off some camping gear these guys, so-called buddies, said they needed and when the whole cop thing went down, he was scared out of his 19 year old mind. He went to jail that night and I thought I would die.

Next day, everyone said I needed a good lawyer, and maybe not from Madera. But I didn't know anyone. My neighbor came right over and plunked down Paul's card. She said he had helped her mother on a trumped up fraud case in L.A. And that he was good, really good. I had no time to research; I called him that morning. After I explained how I got his name and number, he said to wait one hour while he cleared up some deskwork and that he would call me back.

Right, I thought. Bye bye. But he did. And he listened and asked some questions. When I said I was done, he was sort of quiet for a minute and then he told me he'd come up, just to check this all out.

"When can you do that?" I was trying not to cry.

"Larry still in jail? I'm coming up right now."

Well, I started to cry and couldn't get a grip on myself. And he did get Larry out and the trial came months later and Paul knew it was a set up deal and got it all settled. Larry went back to Fresno State and graduated in Psychology. Now he teaches high school. Paul never charged us a dime."

Knots started unraveling inside Marian and she became aware of her breathing. It felt good. As she did in her yoga class, she scanned her body. Her head felt ok, her back relaxed, tension poured out of her clenched arms and legs. And her heart, which had not deserted her, beat.

Georgeanne looked past Marian to the dusty fields beyond the house, fallow for the next crop.

"Sometimes, good people just do good things. It seems nutty these days, but it does happen. Paul was one of the good ones and I was lucky to have him help our family.

That's all it was. You have nothing to worry about, OK? He just helped and kept track of all this awful shit until it was signed, sealed, and delivered.

Does that help you some?" Georgeanne sat quietly, waiting, wondering.

Marian fingered the envelope in her pocket, the one left in Paul's briefcase. All that had been in it was this address and a note that said   "Did Georgeanne know Tim Brewster. Did Larry know him? Check Fresno/Madera records." None of that made sense, but the most critical question was now answered. The other names must have been random links to the case he was trying to ready for court.

Georgeanne broke into her reverie

"Do you need that photo?"

"No. No, you keep it. He'd like to know he was with your family, I think.

Good luck to all of us in the election. Bush has to go. There's not one good thing in his stupid head."

Georgeanne laughed. "Well, you got that right. We can hope. And I am so sorry for your loss. You take care, all right?"

Six hours later, Marian pulled into her Westlake driveway. She sat looking at the dark house for a minute."What now? Is this where I'll always be?" Exhausted, she fell into bed sans husband, sans dog, sans worry. She slept.

Before she drifted into sleep she told herself, "Tomorrow. I'll sort things out tomorrow."

6 Come

"She had been forced into prudence in her youth, she learned romance as she grew older: the natural sequence of an unnatural beginning." Anne Elliot in **Persuasion** *by Jane Austen*

October 25, 2008
On Marian's computer:

Hi Marian,
   I've tried to reach you at home and on your cell, but my info may be out of date. Where are you? I've been worried about you and so is Cara. I know you've been in a fog since Paul died and I want you to know I love you. Too many years apart, but still, you are my cousin and I miss you.

Something has happened here and I
have an idea for you and Cara. I'm
selling the house! No, really, I am
this time. I know I've dithered back
and forth for a long time, but I
know I have to now. The roof is a
wreck, the septic tank is iffy,
everything I can see needs paint---
so many large jobs of repair and I
just can't do it alone.

    Anyway, could you come for
Christmas? It would be our last on
the rock and we'll have a good time.
Cara is coming. Please say you'll
come to the island for a cousins'
Christmas.
    Call when you get in from wherever
you are.
Love,
Norah

    Around 5:00 that afternoon, Marian slipped
Nelly's leash off as the dog wriggled free to dash
inside. A splash of strong purple and orange raged
across the sky in a California sunset making
silhouettes of her two favorite palm trees just
across the way. The moment stretched out until
purples shifted to grey, to black.

Another dusk. Days had dribbled away with meetings and classes taking up Marian's energy and concentration. Good students, some in over their heads, one, incredibly, cheating on her Master's thesis. Marian had spent more time researching the plagiarism and turning the case over to the college provost for adjudication than the unfortunate, soon-to-be-dismissed student had spent "writing" the damn thing.

After the funeral, Marian decided to keep her sabbatical open but fill in for the fall semester while her friend in Art History, Pat Redmond, needed help during a problematic pregnancy. It was shaky going, returning to campus to averted eyes, awkward welcomes and many sympathetic gestures. Still, it was pattern and routine.
She wasn't sure about the coming holidays,dreading being brave and alone.

As Marian ploughed through the piled up e-mails that evening, she deleted without reading almost all of them. Then she opened Norah's. The three of them on the island one last time. That sounded melancholy but it still filled her with childish glee.
Family. A tree. Drinks and laughter. And a sweet goodbye to that house by the sea.

Yes. She'd go.

Before she changed her mind, she hit reply and tapped out:

```
"In a word, yes!  Call later with
exact time.  Looking at arriving Dec.
21.  I'm sure you'll be happy to
move on to something wonderful,
Norah.  So-- it will be the three
graces for Christmas.
Love you,

  Marian
```

Earlier that day, Norah smiled as she checked over the e-mail to Marian and hit "send" firmly. That felt right. As right as finally getting out of the old house on Shelter Island which truly was falling down around her. Thirty years of loyal caretaking to a demanding father and particular mother while still working as a rare book consultant had left her pulled inside out, drained, done.

She looked up from the computer screen and out the window onto Peconic Bay. No summer sailboats skimmed by and the trees, so full and green in summer, were stripped, bare. Bare ruin'd choirs where late the sweet birds sang. Shakespeare's sonnet rang true. The red-winged blackbirds on the deck rail ruffled their feathers against the chill. Tiny black and white chickadees jostled each other for the seeds Norah had sprinkled outside. "Crisp, " the tourist literature would say, not acknowledging that it was a precursor to toe and soul numbing cold for the long, lonely winter.

"Well, I've endured the last one of those," Norah thought, reaching for her coffee in the Irish mug she favored. "I'll need to haul down some decorations with the girls coming. Better get a start on that now."

She pulled down the ceiling ladder to go to the attic and once up there, the past was all-present. Boxes, sleds, skates, quilts, broken furniture--- Norah willed herself to ignore it all only picking up the three boxes she had labeled "Christmas."

Down the ladder and in front of the fire, she opened the first one. Her childhood ornaments looked back—tiny handprints, her lucky duck with the green ribbon around its neck, stars, balls. Looking at years of mementos, dolls still and staring, Norah reflected.

It hadn't all been bad, Norah conceded, but those parents had ultimately drained all spirit from her.

Margaret Mary Lynch and Joseph Bacher. She was Irish and he was German, the dark to her sunny light. Margaret quavered in his shadows and demands, always deferring to him. Except, I remember her standing up to him for me—to buy me dresses for high school, to let me have friends over, to stop nagging me to play the piano.

"Let the girl be," she'd say firmly with an arc to her voice that brooked no rejection.

Norah's memories drifted in like the island fog.

I was kept close to that rambling house in a small village by the sea and as years went by it was clear I would not wander far or leave with any young man. I was to be a home girl. Brief romances sparked up only to die quickly out. Letters to traveling college boys eventually stopped coming. And I took care of this reclusive couple.

Jesus, that sounds like Dickens! So scant. Thin, sad.

Well, no doubt there are huge chunks, gaps, a puzzle lacking the simple satisfaction of feeling the last piece slide into place. Once I took my job at Mahlers Rare Books after studying the history of books, bookbinding, literature and more, life picked up and I still have a wide circle of friends both men and women. Even a few "significant others" over the years.

I don't remember back to when I was truly tiny, but Mom and Dad said the story on Shelter Island started when I was a little bigger, maybe 5.

This life had its joys, too, though.
Norah mentally began to tour the island.
I loved this island. When the South Ferry smacks into place at the dock, chipped white paint flecked off by summer heat and winter storms, you know you're here. Home. The ten-minute ferry ride always decompressed me when I'd been off-island and calmed me for whatever was to come if I were leaving Shelter Island.

Turning up North Ferry Road past the tennis courts, leaning right toward the Heights, tidy Victorians fluffed lacy curtains winked at me, settling fussily in the windows.

Slide into a curbside parking spot when the summer people finally left. Into the small pharmacy with single rows filled with the simplest necessities. Ice cream fountain and cool marble counter. Milkshakes poured from icy metal cups, sweat pooling on the worn counter. A simple tuna on toasted rye made as only Cindy did.

The church is just past the fire station, up the hill to the right. Beyond that, the homely golf course, rutted, weed hazards everywhere, gopher holes, but with a startling view of the Peconic on good days. I had walked that course with Dad many times.

Down below, the ice pond tucked in a hollow on the left. Bike down West Neck Road and now you see more bay, grand lady beach houses on solitary hills, watching you coast by as so many others have. They reserve judgment.

Deer- filled woods of pine and oak near Brander Parkway thicken every year. Breathless pauses when a doe stands with her fawn, just off the road, elegantly gazing, ears pricked for that fine line between safety and danger. She does not run; you are blessed. This is my island.

All of a sudden, you are in front of my house on Peconic, the home my father built with his own two rough hands. Meant as a summer cottage, it never was clever, never sought praise for architectural distinction. Humbly, it sat overlooking thickets of wild berries, brambles, and hedgerows harboring rabbits, deer, and my greatest love, the birds. They fly here all year long and know they are safe, will eat.

On another island finger you could go to Mashomack Nature Preserve and the most carefully guarded birds are there. It's a leafy cathedral and since I don't go to church, my own place of worship.

Norah's interior monologue stopped and she threw on a sweater, suddenly needing to see the beach. Her beach. She walked down the sea grass path onto her beach. This particular spot would be very hard to leave.

The sky was very blue. Cloudless.

A short pier stood in the bay, covered with lichen, years of encrusted shells and seaweed hung in pale greenish-brown bubbled strips. Seagulls careened in with knowing eyes, scanning the shallow waters for unsuspecting fish. A covey of sandpipers scuttled past, clearly on a non-nonsense mission. The waves arched into nicely rounded swells of clear frothy water, inching over the orange and pink and yellow shells covering the beach, the jingle shells of her childhood now displayed in jars throughout the house.

One hopeful grey gull sidled up to Norah.

"You, my friend, are S.O.L. Nothing. Nada. But you are cute."

"Not even a cracker?" the gull rejoined. Then, a deep laugh. Norah's neighbor, Tim, from down the road was ready to cast out for fish.

"Hey, so I talk to birds. I think they like it." Norah walked over closer to the husky 40 year old, a friend for a long time.

"Where's Seamus? Scouting around?"

"No, up at the house. I just needed to clear my head in a dog-free zone for a bit."

"What's up?

"Tim, I think I'm going to sell the house. I haven't told anyone yet. I haven't even said the words out loud. But I'm going to."

"Well, shit. I'll miss you. It's a sweet property all right, but I know the upkeep's something fierce, especially with winter coming on."

They looked out at a nice set of low waves in silence. The sandpipers dug furiously, worrying their way along the pebbly shore. Off to the right, a drifting fog started its slow path around the island neck.

"Days like today, all clear and blue and perfect make it so hard to go. But I have to."

Tim put his arm around her shoulders. "Well, you let me know when the house is good to go. I've got a friend in the city who'd like to be here. Not sure about the house, but..." he trailed off.

Norah laughed. "Oh, I know. Anyone with a million dollars to buy would tear the wreck down and start over. Should, really. And build a second floor to live with my view all the time."

The two were silent and just looked out at the gulls.

"Let's have a drink together before it all gets going, ok?" Tim looked over at her, smiling.

"For sure."

Tim loped off down the beach, pole in hand, seeking a better fishing ground, and Norah turned up the path overgrown with high sea grass, a plank covering the muddy bit, and walked up to her house, looking at it from the sea's point of view.

Simple. Plain. Direct. Brave.

Just like me. For sure, just like me, Norah thought with certainty, climbing the steps to the outer deck behind her home.

The afternoon sun shimmered through the almost bare trees. She turned her face to the warmth. Sun settled on her left cheek. She closed her eyes and just listened.

Red-winged blackbirds pecked at the deck at scattered sunflower seeds. Chickadees scolded each other in a nervous line scratching for tinier seeds.

And the waves churned in.

Then Norah turned, went inside, and e- mailed Marian.

Shelter Island at the east end of Long Island, New York

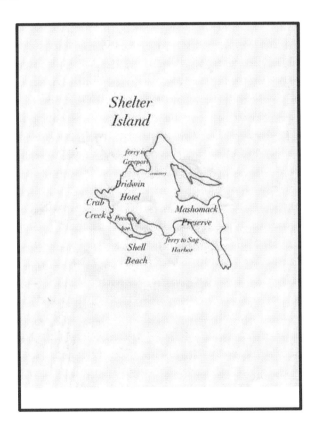

7 First Arrival

December 21, 2008

Shelter Island was losing the sun as the ferry lurched into the pilings at the dock. Gulls rushed up and away, circling the boat, eyes peeled for snacks. They settled onto the piling posts, waiting. Orange glints of light swept the horizon westward toward Quogue, slipped into purple and finally slate.

Marian collected her bag, purse, buttoned the top button on her pea coat and looked through the twilight for Norah's car. On the train out from New York City, she had wondered about this visit and what time with her long-lost cousin would bring. Her island memories were scattered and few, mostly about the shells all over the beach, running with dogs and aunts and uncles watching over gin and tonics.

Walking off the ferry from Greenport, squeezing past three cars, she peered into the parking lot and there was Norah, auburn curls blowing around her fair face, hand raised to wave.

"You're here! And you look grand—get in. Right on time." Norah started up her Audi, trying not to stare full on at her cousin.

"Not much traffic out here in December. Definitely not like the summer lines for the ferry. The rock is pretty empty in the winter." Norah rattled on. "That's one of the reasons I've decided to sell. But let's get you back to the house and fed before we talk about all that." The women settled in the dark, talking, laughing, and tumbling over each other's words, comfortable together as each remembered being in the past.

Years were erased and they were girls again.

Weaving through the now pitch-black woods, Norah turned into Peconic Avenue and the old house sat waiting for them, lights on. The car crunched over the gravel and they were home.

"Oh, Norah, it is good to see the house again. How are the critters?"

"Come see. The cat is Ashley and I think you remember Seamus."

Inside the front door a large orange cat sat expectantly, one paw raised.

"Ashley! What a pretty girl! Come here, kitty." Ashley wound around Norah's legs first, looked speculatively at Marian and then graced her with the same affectionate twirl of belly and tail, marching off with a flourish.

"That's a good cat, Norah."

"Indeedy." Looking around the dining room, she found no more animals. " There's one more around somewhere, but Emily is shy. She'll come out soon. Not sure about their future. I seem to sneeze all summer with them."

Then Seamus exploded from the kitchen, his rich black coat shining, looking fierce as he collapsed on the floor, belly up, begging for a rub.

"Seamus! You handsome devil. What a good boy!" Marian gave him the expected belly scratch. "I bet you'd like to play with my Nelly someday. Mmm. What's that I smell?"

"Boef Bourgignon with fresh bread. OK?" Norah moved swiftly around her tiny kitchen, easily assembling all she needed.

"Fantastic. I was hoping you are still cooking." Marian looked around the kitchen, thinking—this is a home. Everything works in here.

Stepping up to her stove, Norah threw back "I love it. Good to have someone to share it with tonight. Sometimes I get carried away with my recipes and then pack up my freezer. You and Cara are in for some good meals, I hope."

Norah splashed some cabernet into the bubbling pot, poured more into two wine glasses and patted a kitchen chair.

"Sit. Now we can really talk."

"First a toast—to you, the old house, and Christmas!"

They drank appreciatively, taking in the moment, the aromas.

"When is Cara getting here?"

"In two days. So, weather permitting, we can cruise around the island, explore the North Shore a bit and there's a great winery I want you to see."

"Goodie. God, I haven't seen Cara in so many years. How did we all lose touch?"

Norah took a sip of her wine. "Easy enough to do, right? Life just piles up. I know I kind of lost track when she went to Italy and it was letters, now e-mails. I think she is glad to be finding us again."

"Lots of stories, that's for sure."

"Ready to eat?"

"Always, I'm afraid."

More wine, tender beef with baby onions and carrots, crusty fresh bread— life was good, just this very minute. After dinner, dishes done, Christmas music came from the living room radio and they moved to the fireplace with brandies in hand.

Marian snuggled under a soft, blue Irish wool throw, took in the room and sipped her drink. On one wall hung a Japanese silk painting on a long canvas. Small children looked at fish in tanks, parents bent over considering buying them, shops filled with people in a small village somewhere in Japan. It was a wedding gift to Norah's mother from her boss, J.J. Robinson of Morton House Publishing. It drew Marian in on every childhood visit to the island.

Once again she walked into that village, watched the fish, and wondered if the children would play with her in some magical way. It probably was time spent with this painting and many other good prints scattered through the house that ultimately had led Marian into art history. That great release of entering a world of paint, on a flat surface, filled with life, completely real and true.

"I love that painting," Marian said softly.

Norah looked at it with her. "I remember, now, how you would sit and look and look. It will have to live on a new wall now."

"I can see beyond my hazy memories, Norah, and I know the house has major problems. Tell me what's up.

"It's such a relief to talk this out with you. One day, I'm ready to pack up and go, go, go and the next I figure out a hundred ways to find the money to finance and fix her up. Here's one of the balance sheets."

The cousins poured over typed pages of doleful facts: Needed—new roof, wall rot, damp nastiness in the basement, new septic tank and system, major grounds work, warning letters from the island harbor board about dock refurbishment.

"Jesus. You'd need at least $300,00."

"Too right. And that's not for even one pretty thing like new kitchen wallpaper, building that second story, new linens, a flat screen TV...she trailed off.

"It's too much. And add to that the winter loneliness, a life built around a ferry schedule and, and, well, it's just me doing all this shit. For just me."

"OK. So what options look better?" Marian adopted a professional, rational tone.

"The book work is demanding at Mahlers in Manhattan and I love the new director. She trained at Oxford and in Dublin and did some work in Chicago, too. She is very smart, funny and has a good eye for books we need and can sell. So, that keeps me in the city most of the time right now, with a chance to travel to London or Paris each year for viewing possible sales and then tempting our best buyers with new treats we find. The can see them digitally, but still love seeing the embossed covers, touching the leather, touching the pages. No Kindle people here.

Marian considered this. "So will you move to Manhattan? Or Brooklyn?"

"That costs a bloody fortune, too. I like trees and country life a lot, but the commute is nuts. I did have one thought. I don't know, though...." her voice trailed off uncertainly

"What? Try it out on me."

"Well, I have been thinking about a bed and breakfast." She rushed on in a torrent:

"You know, just little. A small house with a few rooms set off for myself. Open for weekends and holidays only. Very private and I could open or close as I pleased. Sort of "Holiday Inn" with Bing Crosby—you know?? Maybe some specialty weekends. A wine lovers winery tour, a book lover's weekend with an author. Anyway." She paused and took a breath.

"Norah, that is just fantastic! With your great cooking it would be a hit. Go for it! I will come all the time!"

"You're the first one I told. It feels more real to have it out there in real live words."

"What about the rare books?"

"It might fit in if I worked it seasonally. Also, I want to go up the Taconic and look in some of those little towns along the Hudson so I could still commute." Suddenly, Norah could see the inn materialize.

"I wish I had a sense of direction like that. I know I am just drifting right now and I can't see very far ahead."

"Let it be. You are here now and that was a big change in itself. You will know what to do. Kind of exciting to think there is a path waiting, somewhere, and it will be the right one. There was a prayer I remember that said something about knowing you are just where you are meant to be. Try it on."

"Thanks, Norah. Christmas on the island was a good idea."

Soon the cousins drifted off to bed, listening to the water lap at the shore just below the thicket of brambles, the thicket where mother deer hid their fawns until they felt safe enough to come right up to the door and munch tomatoes and roses in the summer. Black night. Waves. Sleep.

8 December 22

Coffee aroma drifted up to the turret where Marian slept. Her eyes opened to bright blue sky, whitecaps on the bay, far out to the South Shore and a few brave fishing boats bobbing along. Gulls swooped over the boat channel and settled on the pilings to think.

"What time is it, "Marian mumbled to herself. "Yikes, it's 9:30! I never sleep that much."

She slipped into her robe and scrambled down the spiral steps into the kitchen and living room.

"Hey." Norah glanced up from yesterday's **New York Times** with a smile**.**

"Hey. I slept."

"Yup. Quiche and apple sausage? Coffee?"

"OK, I love you. Be mine forever."

Norah grinned and poured. "Ah me darlin', sure and amn't those the words I've been yearnin' to hear!!"

They laughed and gobbled down goodies. "So, I want to live in your B&B forever."

"Yeah, yeah, but what about today? What would you like to do?"

"Should we dig into the 'move mode '? "

"No, let's wait for Cara. Then we'll get real and down and dirty."

"OK by me. Let's play today."

"The weather is holding and the prediction is for snow soon, but not today. I was thinking a visit to Mashomack would be good. I want to see the trees and animals in winter and say goodbye. Then we can pick up a Christmas tree in the lot by IGA."

"I forget—what is Mashomack?"

Norah laughed. "Selective memory, my cat. That is where the wasps stung you all over when you were here in '83. We hiked in the nature conservancy one day and you scooted up a muddy hill to see the top and the wasp nest collapsed on your downward tumble."

"THAT was Mashomak? I wasn't much of a baby

sitter for you that day. I still have a fear of bees, wasps, flying stinging guys in general. I remember they were in my shirt, in my pants, and some people took me to a room—where was that?"

"I think it was our rental for that summer. It was on the West Neck road just before the preserve. It was when Dad was beginning to build this house. So I was 10 and you were 25 years old. You had just graduated from Williams College as an art history major."

"I forgive the critters. Let's go."

With the woods stripped of leaves, you could see through the branches as you drove by. The trees became a blur of black and brown. There was space in between, but not enough to really see all the way through. It was like hairs in front of your face. In the preserve, foxes paused and froze, rabbits stopped, birds flew in swirls. The ragged undergrowth threatened paths and all was a beautiful scramble of leaves, roots, the "deep down things" of the Hopkins poem. And quiet. Very, very quiet.

After a two hour ramble, Norah and Marian looked at each other and sort of sighed. "It's good to know this place is here and safe. No McMansions will take over."

"I feel like I was on a retreat. Peace." Marian put up the collar on her jacket and felt the winter cold.
Norah started up the Jeep and suggested, "Want to see the cemetery? Mom
and Dad are there now."

"Of course. I've never been there. That makes this island truly yours; they will always be here. That means more than summer people in and out."

"I know. I like that. Even if I leave, it will be mine."

Up South Ferry Road and over Manahanset Road almost to Dering Harbor, they turned left and these woods led to an open grassy cemetery. Simple and plain, as natural as Shelter Island itself. No fancy monuments, jus low gravestones.

"Here they are, " Norah said. I put some evergreen boughs in the trunk for them. From our trees."

While Norah gathered the branches and pinecones, Marian stood looking down at the two graves.

She remembered the kind couple who had let her run wild as a child, not really knowing how to tame her. They were older than most couples with children and Norah had come to them late in life. A happy surprise, they always said. Mary and Joseph with the one perfect kid, was the family joke.

They built the island house, lived here until they died in their seventies. Norah had cared for them until they died at home, all alone, adjusting her position with Mahlers to part time to do so. It could not have been easy.

"I won't ever have this," Marian realized.

"When Paul died, I had him cremated and kept his ashes. So, there is no place to go to. It seemed right, then, but looking at this, I don't know."

Norah was silent. "Don't beat yourself up on that score. These two were a right problem for me. Not as sweet as you might be thinking, believe me. Still, they led their lives here, and here is where they need to be. I owed them that."

With that she fell silent and arranged the branches, stood up, brushed her hands on her jeans and turned to Marian.

"Lunch at the Prid? The hotel is open for lunches this week."

Wind worked its way up from the bay into the woods and cemetery and the sky lost some blue.

"You're on, but my treat."

"Let's table all worries for now and see what we can think up over Christmas," Marian suggested.

"No argument there."

They circled around to the grand old Pridwin Hotel, facing the bay from its stately height, and enjoyed the Christmas decorations, a chowder lunch by the fire and knew they were fortunate in time and place and company. On the way back to the Peconic Avenue house, they stopped at the IGA Market and chose their tree, but decided to wait for Cara to decorate it. It stood in green splendor by the fireplace, filling the room with the smell of Christmas.

Finally that night after a gorgeous Shelter Island sunset, books in hand, they both yawned at the same time. Laughing, Norah said "Let's get you settled in and maybe a kitty will visit you for a snuggle."

They cleared up for the night, looked out at the light snow, and, glad to be with one another, went to bed.

9 The Third Grace

From the minute Cara stepped off the ferry the next day, Norah knew something was off. True, they had not seen each other in years, but still. Purple dusk dropped over the beach and the ferry departed. The hellos and how are you's died off and the silence in the car was palpable, amorphous holes with inanities dropped in by groping strangers.

Inwardly, each wondered if this was mistake. No turning back now, though.

"I left Marian at the house and she's stirring the dinner pots for us. She's happy you are here."

Cara nodded in the dark. "It has been so long. I think it's been 15 years, but I'm not sure. I remember a few summers when our visits overlapped here and our mothers sitting outside on the back lawn looking over the bay, with cold drinks, laughing. I loved seeing them all together. Marian was the sophisticated teenager to my gawky 9 year old. I thought she was very, very cool."

Rounding Brander Parkway, having driven the long way around, the lights on the porch and smoke rising from the chimney were welcome touches.

Norah half-turned to Cara asking, "Is it the way you remember?"

"Hard to say in the dark, but it feels familiar. I remember that split log fence."

"Well, let's get you in and something hot to drink. I see Marian waiting at the door."

The car crunched over the gravel and as the door to the house opened, Seamus bounded out, wriggling with joy to see Norah.

"Hey, big guy! This is Cara. Say hello like a well-trained puppy."

Seamus jumped up to Cara to put his front paws on her shoulders, gave her a slobberly kiss, and for the first time, Cara laughed.

"God, he has no manners at all," apologized Norah.

"That's ok. I love dogs and he's a beaut. Not like those frou frou city dogs prancing around my neighborhood."

"In, in, in everybody. It's freezing!"

Bags in, Marian hugged Cara hello and everyone sized each other up amidst coats, offers of a drink, and plans for dinner.

Marian thought to herself...Pretty. Sandy colored short-cropped hair, flashing eyes, a muscular but slender body. A cat not relaxed yet, but with a tentative easiness.

Norah couldn't think as she checked the beef bourguignon. Hope this was not a huge mistake. She looks nice but very wary. And pretty with a real dancer's body.

Scotch in hand, taking small sips, Cara surveyed her family in this house from long ago. It's like a fairy tale, in a way. Why am I here? But the flight impulse went away and she began to relax. She admired the great rusty red hair on Norah, who was a small bundle of energy with startling blue eyes. At home and eager to share.

Marian? Bit of a cipher there. Tall, mixed dark brown and grey hair in an attractive bob cut, framing a round face with hazel eyes, a softness to her.

Voices came in a blur. "Sorry? Dreaming here," explained Cara.

"Let's eat. " The tiny kitchen table filled with hot bread, the simmering beef, red wine and a toast to cousins. The newly constructed family ate by candlelight and stayed on fairly innocuous conversation about Christmas, travelling, snow. Dinner finished, Cara said quietly,

"Look, I hope you don't mind, but I think I'm going to crash early tonight. The past week has been nuts and I'm beat."

"Well, of course you are. We'll visit more tomorrow. Let me show you your room. It's the one facing the bay so you can fall asleep with the waves."

Cara waved goodnight as she walked down the hallway and Marian and Norah looked at each other.

"Something is just not right," Marian murmured and Norah agreed.
"I know, but it will come out. Let's sleep on it."
So they did.

10 December 24 Christmas Eve

Christmas Eve dawned with a blue sky and high clouds moving across the horizon with a brisk wind. Coffee, raspberry croissants and scrambled eggs lured Cara and Marian into the kitchen.

"Merry Christmas Eve, ladies," smiled Norah. "Hungry?"

"Famished." Marian plopped down with a plateful of food. "Cara, you'll have to tell us about any dancer's diet rules you have."

"OK, but they're pretty much suspended for Christmas."

Over coffee and more rolls, each cousin offered her history to the other two as a summary of years passed separately. In the abbreviated form, Norah chronicled the years of island life caring for her parents, traveling back and forth from the city, tending a rare book business online as much as possible.

"I'm ok, really. It's not a tragic life, but I think I have to move on now without this shambles of a house slowing me up. I'll give you the not-so-grand tour later and you'll see what I mean."

Marian nodded in understanding. "Houses can be anchors; sometimes dead weights. Paul and I decorated ours when we moved in and left it. We thought we'd be re-doing parts for children, but that didn't happen. I wasn't one to fuss and change often. With both of us working, it became our frame, both a jumping off point and a return haven, too. It's much younger than yours, of course, but I know when you have a broken something, a leaky roof, everything else takes a back seat to that."

"Will you stay there now with Paul gone?" Cara asked.

Marian's eyes filled, surprising her. "I just don't know what to do." She looked out the window at the skies getting greyer.

"I've felt that way, sometimes. The answer will come. One dance instructor had an expression about 'mental soak.' Just put your idea or question in your mind and leave it alone. Sooner rather than later, an answer comes. It's miraculous, really."

She smiled at Marian and saw her cousin nod. Marian looked gratefully at Cara and all three women considered the possibilities in that advice.

Norah looked out the bay window to the far part of her cove and when she turned back, it was with an idea.

"Let's walk. We'd better get out now and try to get to Shell Beach and back. Those clouds mean business. We might have a white Christmas, girls!"

Scarves, gloves, Seamus on leash and they set off the narrow road to the east to Shell Beach. Silent houses watched them move down the road, their owners gone for the winter. Eight geese flew in a V overhead. Mice and rabbits scuttled through bare bracken, cloaked in its grey web of thorns and branches.

The silence was awesome.

"I've never been here in winter," murmured Marian, her voice muffled by the wind.

Glancing at Norah, Cara added, "You really are alone off-season, aren't you?"

Norah looked around, aware of what they saw in cold desolation. "Yes. I'm used to the silence, but more and more I need voices. People."

They walked on. Whitecaps played on the bay and gulls swooped down for any surface fish. Chickadees pecked at a low berry bush, gleaning seeds and dried fruit. White clouds grew heavier.

"I smell snow," Cara smiled.

They moved in companionable silence; Cara's pace quickened as they turned right to the bank of sea grass leaning toward the water.

"Shells!! I remember these from all those summers ago!"

Thin pink, yellow, orange translucent shells mingled with grey and white striped scallop shells. Pierced conch shells mutely recalled gulls breaking in for the meat. Mussels and oyster shells stayed glued to seaweed. A lovely, untouched display, this.

Shivering, the women sat on the sandy bank, wrapped in drifting thoughts.

Finally, Cara spoke in a low voice, looking directly out to sea, eyes fixed on her own horizon.

"There are some things you don't know about me," she began. "But it's too cold to start my story here. Let's go back." Curious and cold, the three women returned to the house.

11 By the Fire

With tea, Christmas cookies homemade by Norah, the fire settling into itself, everyone gathered in the living room, chairs facing out to the now very windy bay. Questions were muted.

Cara look nervous. She had some papers in her hand and sat on the far couch, looking up finally.

"I have a grant application here. It's not even a rough draft. But I think I want to read it to you instead of trying to figure out how to really start." She swallowed. Norah and Marian smiled in encouragement.

"A grant in dance!! How great for you. Let's hear it."

Cara just did not know these women inside and out. She had no idea where this story would lead the three of them, but it was time to tell her tale. She had a complete life and persona off this little island, but, in the circumscribed group of her tiny family, she was uncertain.

She began.

To the Glendower Foundation for the Humanities

Preliminary Letter

In 500 words, describe your proposal including any relevant background making this project particularly appropriate for New York City.

Well, Jesus. That's a lot of words. I haven't written this kind of thing in years. I'm just going to set everything down in some sort of order and fix it up later. God knows therapists have been telling me to do this for years; only they weren't offering me money at the end of the story.

I've been laid off from the Martha Graham Dance Company long enough that severance pay, odd jobs, and adjunct dance instruction just isn't squeezing together enough. I need cash. And, I really do have a grand idea. I think Graham will have me back next season once my leg really heals. I have to think about where it all started, though.

I'm pretty sure I was the only dyke at the prom back in Stonebraker, Kansas. Yep, pretty sure about that. The guy who asked me to be his date for the Senior Prom at the Cherry Valley Country Club was nice enough, I guess, and pretty clueless.

But so was I. I always wanted to move and dance. Mom got me every pink, fluffy tutu the Emporium stocked, but I would take off the frou frous, get down to skirt and tights, and dance. To **Shake, Rattle and Roll**. To **Sleeping Beauty**. To **Sound of Music**. To the theme from TV shows. Go. Move.

When Wilma Longfeather moved into town and opened her studio, she was pretty cheap to start with and Mom marched me over to her and sort of left me on her doorstep.

"This one won't stop dancing, so I guess she needs some real lessons." Mom looked me over as an interesting specimen.

Wilma's eyes ranged up and down over my slim frame, chucked me under my 10-year-old chin and looked way into my green eyes.

"Hmm. Yes. I can see she has the nice long body, legs, and something else in those green eyes. What do you think, little lady?"

I peeked into the small studio and I thought I'd found heaven. Music. Mirrors. Long rails. Smooth, wooden floors.

"Yes, please. I'd like to try."

Wilma was Sioux. Her studio sign was one feather. That's it. She was six feet tall and had dark brown skin, blazing black eyes and took no crap from anyone. She lived alone, I figured out later, for a long time, and she was happiest when she strode into the middle of the studio, raised her arm and declaimed, "And one!" to gawky girls.

No boys showed up. Too gay, I guess.

You know the scene in Billy Elliott when he just flies to the music and takes it out on rooftops and into the street? That was me.

After a while, I tuned into ballet and modern dance blends. Wilma pushed, prodded, made me repeat move after move until I cried, all the while watching me, fixing me tea after the others left, making sure I did my homework, too. I loved her.

I pretty much lived there and collapsed at home. Mom and Dad looked at me like a racehorse they couldn't quite figure out where to bed down. "You are my 'rara avis,' Dad said. "My own sweet rare bird that needs to fly away."

The "away" part came later. When I was a senior, Wilma had prodded me into applying to Juilliard, a school in New York I had never heard of.

February 1991 I walked into the main rehearsal room at Wilton Studios in Chicago for local tryouts for Juilliard first year students. Mirrors. Barre. Floor. Beat up piano. So far, I recognized the arena. But this was sharper, keener from the first note. Everyone was so good. Tall, young women. Slender, gracefully arching backs. Supple bodies. Tatty exercise warmers. Handsome, lithe young men, all arms, all legs, all colors—and all serious and ready to fly. Later, I realized they were as frightened as I was. I danced my heart out that day and luckily, it was good enough. In a few weeks I got the word that I was accepted at Julliard. I couldn't afford to go, though, and put the idea on hold.

When I told Wilma the good news, she said, "I know. I was reading my Bible today and a page fell out."

Cara put the sheaf of papers down and looked at her cousins.

"So. That's me. Or at least the start of who I am now."

Norah opened a bottle of Domain Chandon wine. "A special California wine for someone special. I believe that would be you!" Glasses clinked and the simple acceptance of her story and her self opened an unexplored part of Cara's heart.

Marian leaned toward Cara, glass in hand. "I can see why you might have been unsure about our reactions, but I hope you see now that we have all grown up. We aren't the little conservative Catholic girls we were when we met on summers with our moms. For that matter, I don't think we' re even Catholic anymore...are we?"

The question hovered in the Christmas Eve air. The Spirit of Christmas Past lingered to hear the answer.

"I checked out a long time ago," Norah started. " I remember going to crown Mary in May and wanting to be in processions. I remember incense and loving it, especially as the censor would swing back and forth. I loved the Mass, the priests, even Sister Gerardus who started out by scaring the living bejesus out of me in the second grade at St. Raymond's.

I think it all went south when I realized all I ever, ever saw were men up there. No women. The nuns, yeah, but no girls like me anywhere. I signed up to be an altar boy one year and the nun just laughed at me and sent me back to my classroom. I couldn't figure out why.

Later, I went to the local public schools, Columbia, and I stopped trying. Now, the abuse of all those little boys has sealed the deal for me. So, I don't know...I guess I pray looking at this bay. I do believe in God, just not the one the Pope likes."

Marian took up the line of conversation. "I know it was a big deal for our mothers, but I just went along. I loved the stained glass, the statues. I guess that got my art history mojo in gear. And now I can't get enough of Celtic art, the manuscripts, all things ancient Irish. But I never felt holy back in the day; I hated counting up sins, and when I just stopped going to Mass, Mom and Dad let it go. Maybe they were going through the motions themselves. I liked wearing lacy mantillas, though. Can't leave that out!"

"Well, that's not much to go on is it? " Cara looked at her cousins, taking in this reality.

"As a lesbian, I am a non-starter for the Catholics. Evidently, God screwed up in making me this way and so I can only get to heaven if I try very, very hard not to do any queer things. You know, like falling in love with a woman, having sex with her, growing old with her." Suddenly her eyes filled and she caught her breath.

"That church put me out and I am fine without it." This last was final and definite.

"Soooo, Norah inquired, "I am guessing that we are not on for Midnight Mass?"

They laughed, but each felt a tinge of loss, a twinge.

"No, no Mass, but I think we are finding a way to be real, to really share each other, and I don't know what to call that. But, you know what? It feels holy and I like it."

Marian poured the last of the champagne and each silently clinked the Waterford crystal goblets.

In unison they said, with feeling, "Amen."

12   Christmas Day

That night it snowed.

Soft, tentative flakes at first, building to a thick massy net of dense snow, falling silently for hours. The few lights within sight glimmered and winked.

In the morning, the wee hours of Christmas, Norah led Marian and Cara up to the attic, claiming more dusty boxes of Christmas ornaments to place on the waiting tree.

"One last tree! Let's make her a pretty one," she called down from the attic.

"What we don't use, we can throw out after I say goodbye to them. I have more in the living room already. " The boxes got passed down hand to hand.

"OK." Marian dug in. "No artistic theme? Just— 'I like it all?' "

"Your motifs will have to appear some other time, my dear. This tree will be loaded and hokey." Norah looked around speculatively.

The attic hid boxes of dishes, linens, old chairs, stacks of forgotten pictures and paintings, books galore, old toys, albums, skates, blankets and assorted flotsam and jetsam from several maiden aunts and widows. Why it had all ended up in this musty attic on an island was a mystery, but Norah's mother had become the repository of family mementos and photos collected and passed down for over one hundred years. She had the stories. They were all in here, somewhere.

"Look!" Cara held up a box labeled "Family Photos/Docs." "Let's go through it downstairs. Maybe we are all richer than we dreamed!"

"I don't think so." Norah wrinkled her nose and forehead. "This is just a great big catch-all. I give you to carte blanche in dumping this stuff. Marian, you keep an eye out for any Van Goghs or Antique Roadshow treasure."

Each woman picked up and put down items, went on her own exploration. The attic was quiet. Outside the circle window in the east eave, snow fell and the light for this new Christmas was weak. A bare electric bulb snapped to life and the search went on.

They found:

1 doll, no eyes
1 Teddy Bear, loose foot
a sled
a scratched, brown wooden school
desk, seat attached, ink bottle hole
stained blue
coats
boots with clasps and cords
a fur coat with satin lining
boxes of linens, some with pulled
thread patterns
stitchery samplers
needlepoint
cross stitched napkins
Irish silver

All this and more silently awaited the three cousins on this small island.

They roamed the attic silently, ghosts swirling around them, hands reaching out to touch theirs. They did not hear the silent sighs of frustration, joy, surprise, agony, desire in the dusty air.

One silent voice remembered her wedding breakfast, then a toast with Guinness beer in the garden, she in a long flowing, clinging satin gown; he smart and handsome smiling at the camera.

Another old one saw her mother's tablecloths all stitched in green cross stich. One was to go to every daughter. Had they arrived?

A man long gone sensed someone touching the love letters he had sent. Why were they here now and who was looking at them? It did not matter, he guessed.

How to begin?

Norah decided. "OK, take what you can hold of papers and photos and we'll sort out the rest of this lot after Christmas. Let's have breakfast by the fire and have a look see."

Norah

She sifts through the box labeled "Norah" as a logical starting point. Amidst baby shoes, a child's blue woolen cap, a tiny wooden truck is a dusty, brown folder labeled "Dublin." She opens the file and steps into a new past---her own. She fingers a photo of a priest in front of a church. He opens an envelope addressed to her mother and father with a Dublin return address. The letter inside stated simply that

This is to verify the final adoption of girl, age 2, hair: blonde, eyes: blue, weight 30 pounds, height 3 feet. Child identified herein as Norah. Adoptive parents: Joseph and Margaret Mary Brach of East Rockaway, New York, United States of America.

This female child was an abandoned baby accepted by the Sisters of Mercy in Dublin, St. Patrick's Home. Child left at this mother and baby home in January 1968 by a young woman of St. Catherine Parish in Birr, Offaly. The woman was of good health and known to me. Birth record recorded as Ann Malone, Mother Ellen, father unknown.

Father James McIntyre

St.Patrick's Mother and Baby Home. April 19, 1970

Cara

One box intrigues Cara. Tied in ribbons, sere and frayed, are letters. Packets of letters. Postcards from summers long ago. Envelopes with faded stamps and ink. Names she has never heard before. Friends? Relatives? No way to know now. Just enjoying the beautiful scripts in flowing fountain pen inks, she fingers the packets. Tucked under a green ribbon on one is a calling card. A calling card!! In copperplate script it announces "*Kathleen Lynch. June. 1955.*"

My mother, Cara breathes. Mom. She was graduating in 1955. Cara opens the letter collection, not speaking. Everyone fades away; the only sound she hears is the fire and her heart.

Eyes racing over the words, no sense. Names never heard of. Who is "Lee?" A boyfriend? His name comes up throughout. Cara slips the letters into her pocket, ready to read them slowly in her room tonight.

Marian

The heat from the flames warms Marian's right side, her face flushed. She feels pink and sips her coffee, watching Cara and Norah reading pages from the past. She picks up a mottled blue leather folder with a gold clasp. It looks like an old diary and she opens it. It is a letter case with pockets for stationery, letters, and a pen. Very sweet and quaint. These letters look very private and she almost puts them aside. They are love letters filled with endearments to "Bill." They are not signed except for "Yours, forever." A true Christmas mystery. Out of one envelope fall several black and white pictures. Small, maybe 3" by 3" with the ruffled white edges from long ago.

Who is looking at me, Marian wonders. This is like seeing paintings in a new museum, faces smiling out from canvas and frames for you to know from afar. In one, a sassy looking couple dressed in slacks and skirts from the 40's, a scarf over the girl's head, her head set back with an open smile for the camera, the man leaning over her with his arm easily, comfortably over her shoulder. They are perched on a large boulder. It is in the countryside, somewhere. Near the blue folder are boxes labeled for birthday gifts to Kathleen from Clare. What had mother given her sister, Marian wondered. A bracelet. A pin shaped like a monkey. Cream gloves. Marian smiled, thinking of the sisters.

A log fell in the fireplace, sparks shooting upward.

As if from far away, Norah, Cara and Marian looked at each other.

Norah began. "Well, this is a lot to take in. Let's talk later, after breakfast and the tree."

13 Gifts

The tree, when completely decorated, looked quite fine. Angels, carolers, lights, ornaments both large and small sat expectantly, waiting for Santa.

All day the snow fell in heavy drifts over the marsh, on the beach, on animal nests, on trees, on the house and up to the door.

Christmas music floated through the warm house and Marian and Cara woke to Irish voices singing and bacon on the griddle. In robes and pajamas they trundled into the kitchen like expectant children.

"Merry Christmas Cara! Merry Christmas Marian! Look how beautiful everything is! So much snow for our white Christmas."

Norah smiled over her coffee. "More snow than we bargained for. Well, we needn't dig out today or even budge. We have everything we need and we can cook all day."

"Are we stuck?" Marian peered out the broad window with California eyes.

"Oh, kind of. They'll probably plow us out tomorrow or the next day. The garage door will open and we can shovel out the driveway, but even a walk sounds impossible until the roads are cleared off."

Cara grinned. "Perfect, then."

Morning cooking occupied the women and soon breakfast appeared on a round table covered in a cheery, red cloth. Pancakes, bacon, coffee, juice, warmed cinnamon apples were gobbled up with laughs and now comfortable silence.

"We are a family." Cara said this with some amazement in her voice. "Really, the only family each of us has."

This sank in.

Norah knew what came next. "Let's open presents and share what we found in the attic!"

They left the dishes and went into the living room by the now bespangled tree.

"Marian—oldest first. Give and tell." Cara wrapped the cashmere throw around her and snuggled into the footstool chair.

"O.K. Here are my presents." Marian looked at them doubtfully. " It was a guess for each of you."

Norah ripped open a small box to find an enameled pin of a Celtic bird in deep blues, greens and crimson.

"It's perfect---more than you know." Her eyes filled with tears and Marian went on.

"Goody. I thought Irish was the key to this Christmas. Open yours, Cara."

Cara opened a larger box to find a book of classic Martha Graham dances in full color photographs.

"**Acts of Light: Martha Graham in the 21st Century**. This is spectacular! I know some of these ballets but not all. I've seen it at Graham and wished for a copy. And it's laid out with such a beautiful sense of open space and photography. Thank you, dear."

"My pleasure. Let's see what my treasures are. 'To Marian from Cara.' She posed by the tree shaking her two presents. Inside an oblong box was a soft leather wallet in a muted, rich, grey. She touched it and looked to Cara for details.

"I studied in Italy some years ago and brought some leather pieces home with me. Now this one is home with you."

Marian hugged her cousin. "I love it."

Norah spoke up with "I hope I got one, too!" And she did.

"My turn." Norah went to the tree and took out her two presents—one in scarlet red for Marian and one in deep green for Cara. "I went rummaging for treasures before you got here and found these. I thought you'd like a part of our past."

Each box held a silver frame, each one slightly different, polished and gleaming.

"They are from Ireland and very old, but I don't know who brought them here. Now they can get to work again for you."

"Well, they are perfect. What a wonderful surprise!" Cara and Marian fingered the clasped hands at the crown of each frame, each pleased.

"Who is in the picture?" Three young girls stood in a photographer's studio, dressed in party dresses from long ago, looking directly at the camera.

Cara smiled and told them to look carefully. These three girls were their mothers. Norah's mother, Margaret Mary stands with a sprig of flowers in her hands, looking somewhat quizzically ahead. Kathleen, Cara's mom, stands squarely, looking into the camera with a blunt, direct gaze. And Clare, Marian's mother, stands to the right, sweet curls framing her face.

"Everyone called them the three graces after the Greek statues. I think they were Beauty, Creativity and Joy. I guess we are the three graces now."

"Time to share the attic secrets now. Oldest to youngest, I think." Cara plopped down on the sofa and looked expectantly at Marian.

Marian acquiesced. "Age, then." She passed a soft,blue leather writing tablet to her cousins. Flecks of pale blue leather fell from the old writing portfolio. The tarnished brass clasp fit snugly into the center, yielding to pressure on the button.

"Isn't is beautiful? It's cracked in spots, but that blue..." Inside were photos.

"I don't know any of the people but I did pick out my mother. It was in a box labeled 'Clare,' my mom. See—there she is, next to the guy with the wavy hair. It's some sort of lake trip. I don't see dad, but maybe he took the picture."

In the black and white photo were six people. Four women, two men in their late teens or 20's. All the girls wore slacks and casual sweaters and the young Clare's curly hair was capped with a soft felt cloche. The two men were in military uniform, army probably. Everyone looked straight at the camera, smiling broadly. One of the women was laughing, mouth open, head cocked to one side.

Handing the blue folder back, Cara lost her grip and it fell to the floor. A piece of cream-colored writing paper now edged its way out and she picked it up. "A letter! Maybe some clues. I feel like Nancy Drew. Let's see..." Looking together, Cara and Marian read the letter aloud to Norah.

Carlton Lodge

August 1946

Dear Kath,

Wish you were here, kid. We're having a great time. These are the Murphy girls and their brothers. Aren't they gorgeous? The guys, I mean. Tim and Bill just got back from duty in Germany and are finally getting out of the army.

Tim is the one next to me. Kath, I think I'm in love! No, really, this time. Don't tell Mom. I'm going to meet Tim in New York and go to the Stork Club!! His unit is having a goodbye dinner dance. I told Mom the Murphy girls are taking me for a shopping trip so I can get a couple of new suits for the next job.

Be a pal and keep my secret?

XOXO,

Clare

P.S. He's a great kisser!!

Marian did some mental calculations.

"Well, Tim must have disappeared because Mom married Dad two years later. Wonder if the romance got going or puffed out when Tim wasn't in uniform. He's sure cute."

Cara rifled through her box, one labeled "private."

"I may have the answer here. It's another letter from Clare dated 1952."

"Read on. Let's find ol Tim." Marian waited for Cara to start.

This note was on lined paper torn from a pad, brittle with age.

"Kath—needed to write. Tom is working on the bills tonight. I was walking down Madison from the office after a late lunch at the luncheonette and bumped right into Tim Murphy at a corner, waiting for the light.

Remember him from that summer years ago? I thought he was "the one" and our little romance was sweet but short. He took a job in D.C. and that was that. Until last Friday.

It was late, pushing four, snow was coming down, and he asked me to get a drink with him at Grand Central before he left town. I don't know why, but I did. We walked to the terminal and he had his arm around me---well, it was snowing and all—and we laughed trying not to fall down.

I kept looking at him. So tall and handsome, dark hair and eyes, a crooked grin.

The city was even quiet with the snow, all the horns and whistles were muted, and it just seemed to get smaller.

We went into the Oyster Bar and Kath, we talked and talked. It was a long visit and it felt good.

I saw him to his train just off the Bar entrance and before it pulled out, he turned and kissed me. On the cheek, but still. And he just looked long and hard at me, and then he was gone.

Kath, I ached inside. I can't do anything, can't tell Tom. I'm probably making some grand thing out of nothing. But way, way down, I think that I have made a mistake. I should have followed him to D.C. years ago.

> *I've missed my chance.*
>
> *Just keep this private and tuck it away.*
>
> *Love you,*
>
> *Clare*

"I never knew any of this." Marian fell silent. The very old news lay on the table, untouched. "Everyone has regrets, missed chances. It just is strange to think of my mother in that situation. It makes me think again about how she and Dad were, really, together. I guess I'll never know." Marian seemed thoughtful more than sad or deeply upset.

After some fresh coffee and Christmas cookies, Cara began her own report on her own mystery.

"Well, in a funny way, my surprise explains a lot to me."

She brought out a photo album of about 20 pages. Black and white photos were glued to black paper in a narrow pocket photo album. Embossed in gold on the white leather cover was one word: "Lee."

Cara began. "Mom used to kid about a "long lost love" she could only be pen pals with. She talked about "Lee" and I always thought it was some guy from high school.

It definitely was not. Lee was a woman and here they are. There were no pictures of her anywhere at home or in Mom's things when she died. Dad mentioned this "Lee" once or twice and just shook his head.

'But she picked **you,** Dad,' I'd laugh.

'Did she, doll? Did she? Then I won!!' and he'd tickle me."

Norah and Marian crowded around to look at the album.

A picture of two girls in their twenties, maybe, arms entwined, cocktails in hand, women in the background.

Silly pictures taken by each of them as the other posed.

Blowing kisses.

Slow, loving smiles.

Sassy poses on the beach.

Funny faces in a photo booth with a string of pictures.

They were lovers.

"Wow." Marian turned the album pages once more, slowly. "So, who knew what in your house?"

"Dad was always ok with me, my choices, my ways and seemed to know more about me than I did. Mom kept her distance and never seemed relaxed with me. She just didn't know what to tell me, I guess. She never came out herself. God, it was 1958. She must have felt so screwed up. And a good Catholic girl, to boot."

No one had words for this.

Outside, the snow fell, lighter than before.

By silent agreement, the women just sat together and Marian took Cara's hand. Norah got up and went into the kitchen and put the waiting turkey into the oven. She came back into the living room and sat down.

"I don't know where to start, " she said calmly.

She put a sheaf of papers on the table, stirred the sparking fire, snuggled the dog even closer and took a deep breath.

"OK ladies, here I go. I'm not who you think I am. Who I think I am. It seems I'm Irish, all right. I was adopted from a Dublin orphanage in 1975 when I was two."

Cara just stared. "You had no idea?"

"None. Not a whisper, not a whit. And those two old fools died never telling me."

Tears fell and Marian joined Cara in a swoop of hugs, good long ones.

"Well, you're still you and you are still ours. Let's figure this out." Marian spread out all the papers, covering the dining room table.

Yellowing papers included a letter from a priest, letters from an orphanage in Dublin, a passport with a child's face peering out, and saved as well was a tiny stuffed horse, baby socks.

"This is huge. It's too much for me, for us, on Christmas. Let's stomp in the snow."

Norah handed out scarves and mittens and boots and thy all bundled up, delighting the dog with his clanking leash, and went out into the drifts, falling, laughing, finding a few open bits to walk until they reached the beach. Here, the wind railed and they all just ran and ran and ran. The dog collapsed first.

This oddest of all Christmases was one each would always remember. Secrets were just beginning to become undone and the women wisely left the mysteries they had opened for later. They ate turkey and drank wine, sang carols, played Scrabble and found quiet corners for naps and reading.

14 Musings

The week between Christmas and New Year's blended into one, long, snowy day. Roads were clear after a few days and each woman spent time alone, walking to the sound of muffled crunches in packed snow, waves hitting the beach as a constant beat. Each was filled with wonder and doubt; this augured well for a new year. Separately the cousins explored the lacunas new information imposed upon them.

On Wednesday, Marian sat on her bed. Strewn about her were photos of Tim and Mom, on the beach, at a picnic, hamming it up for the camera. Matchbooks from cafes. A diary from that summer ending with the entry: " I love this guy, but he is not Catholic and I don't think it will work."

Marian spoke softly to her mother.

"You married the wrong man, Mom. Tim was full of joy and adventure. He loved you and you should have run after him. What did it matter that he was a Protestant? You never made much of being a Catholic. Who would have cared? When he kissed you on that train platform, that was your second chance, your moment, your aria, your glimpse into tomorrow. But the train left, with Tim on it.

But now I know you more. I have become you, I'm afraid. My years with Paul were not the adventure I was meant to have. We took "safe," Mom, when we should have walked the high, trembling bridge through the jungle, walking over treetops. Why were we so afraid? Did we not know how wonderful we were, that we deserved blue and orange and yellow streaks of joy? Why didn't we know we were enough even without children?"

Marian slipped a few of the heartbreaking letters into her pocket.

"I'm just waking up now, Mom, to the power and the beauty I am. I loved Paul so much and I did not let him know, did not make new roads for us. We both could have done more together. Maybe on our Costa Rica trip we would have started over.

But this is a new year, Mom, and I am not looking back."

At pretty much the same time, Cara walked through the woods to Crab Creek and sat on a flat rock, watching the water lap up at the stony shore. And she talked to her mother, too.

She studied the pictures of Kathleen and Lee, looking for clues in every detail.

"Poor you. You seemed so cold and remote to me, but here you are with your soul mate. She looks solid and centered, full of wisdom. You were just too startled, I guess, to let yourself be the woman you were meant to be, in Lee's arms.

Puzzles are solving themselves for me now, Mom.

I think Dad loved you with all his heart, but knew you couldn't return the gift, not fully. And then your queer dyke daughter arrives, mirroring you so much you were shocked and amazed and frightened for me. I wish you could have told me, talked to me. Trusted me. But I think you pulled back trying not to hurt me, hoping I'd find my own way. Dad knew. He always knew and he kept your secret, but he let me fly. How about that?"

Norah did not talk about her adoption to Marian or Cara. When they delicately tried to broach the topic, she shied away with "Not yet. Can't yet." Many emotions rippled through her in waking hours and in sleep. She lost herself in a frenzy of stripping the house down, cleaning with a vengeance. The energy explosion was a welcome channel for all the women as they tried to absorb so much new and disturbing information. They seemed to be facing 2009 in new skins, uncertain of whom they really were.

Norah felt healthy, sloughing off the lies of her battered past. She'd think and plan later. Now was the time for letting go. She enlisted Cara and Marian to pitch boxes from the attic, empty drawers, ransack closets.

"You, my dears, have carte blanche. Throw it all out. If the house sells quickly I want to be ready to go. If you're not sure, ask me or put it in a pile by the piano, which also has to go, by the way. My next life will be away, and smaller. Less is more!"

And they did. The garage was filled with more detritus than could be believed. Margaret Mary had become the repository for furniture, mementos, books, golf clubs, tennis racquets, tools from several generations. Way too much had landed on this island.

Norah laughed just looking at all the crap in one place. "Dear God. The thought that all those people had to haul all this shit here on a boat to get it here and dump it. Unbelievable! Hope that gene passed me by."

"Dump! That's it!" crowed Norah. "We will go to the dump and donate treasures. You won't believe how islanders prowl over that place. I know some of this stuff came from the dump and back it now goes. I predict new homes for lots of this antiques roadshow, not that anything I see has much cash potential. And a big dumpster is coming today."

They dispatched:

Linens

Rotten books
Toys
    A sled (kept)
    A school desk from St Raymond's elementary school, inkwell intact (kept)
    Ice skates (kept)
    Tools
    Cans
    Racquets
    Rosary beads
    Calligraphy calling cards
    Gloves for ladies in soft leather, cotton

**Sewing and embroidery samples
Postcards from long ago vacations
China knick-knacks dogs cats birds
cups houses more more!!
A complete set of Limoges china
(kept)
Irish silver (kept)
Many many lamps
Curtains held together with safety pins
Grocery lists
Receipts for every imaginable
purchase
Tax returns
Cards—birthday, Christmas, sympathy,
on and on
3 lawnmowers—none working
...and so much more.**

They marked New Year's Eve with toasts to the future, to themselves, to the new president. Hope. Change. Change you can believe in. May it be so.

In bed, before falling asleep that last night of the year, each reflected....

Marian

It was the year that Paul's last kiss was on my cheek. He left home in a suit, talking about cell phones, computers. That next week we were supposed to walk with Nelly on our beach in Carmel and watch her roll in the sand. We would laugh at her and brush her out before the sand got in our cottage. But instead of that beach, that water, you smashed your beautiful body in a land-locked town nowhere, dead, in the middle of California.

It was the year I found my family and started looking out instead of always in, in.

*

Norah

It was the year that ancient old woman who pretended to be my mother finally died in the back room of the house. She couldn't hear the sea any more, just humming fans to cool her. It was the year that damned silver bell stopped ringing for me if I didn't scurry down the hall fast enough. No more bells. The leaks and cracks snarled out at me and monsters threatened me from the damp cellar. Everything had to go. All of it. There was no more charm left in those eight rooms.

But the sea—that still charmed me, lulled me, called me. It just was not enough anymore.

Marian and Cara think I have power, drive, that I live alone and in my world all is orderly. I do have direction; you can't say I don't. Things get done without dithering and you just damn well move on. I can still see the sand they tracked into the house on their last day here. No one really sees sand on the floors if you haven't lived here forever and eternally have to sweep it up lest some old woman down the hall carp at you about it. Sand. Some old woman not even my mother. When I think of all the getting and cleaning I did for her. And they kept my aunts in silence, that's for sure. Good secret-keepers in this family. That house is a crumbling wreck. Well, it doesn't matter any more.

*

Cara

It was the year my body failed me. My soul had already started to crumble when Keiko left and I danced as hard as I could to ignore the dissolving part of me that left with her. It was the year I stopped caring about myself, my secrets, my loneliness. I walked into two lives with Norah and Marian and started a new part of my life. I want to dance again. For myself.

15 Unnoticed

Finally, on January 3, Norah lifted her hand in farewell. Marian and Cara left together, having decided to go to New York City and stay together for a while, letting Marian explore the city. Cara would complete her grant application and make the rounds again for fill in work until she was completely healed, and teach at Graham. Both had pledged to help Norah in any adoption research she might choose to begin.

Just two weeks ago, Norah had no idea that this final Shelter Island Christmas would open so many boxes and doors and bring her two cousins to her heart.

The ferryman clanged the gates closed, snapped chains onto the deck, and the ferry grunted into high gear, chugging through the frosty wind across to Greenport.

Norah went to her car, turned on the engine in the January cold, and was finally alone with her thoughts. By the time she'd made it to the golf course and turned down West Neck Road, she was close to the decision that the cleaning work had put at bay.

She took the long way around, following Brander all the way to Shell Beach, stopped the car and got out to tell the gulls and terns what was next. She brought up the wool collar of her coat to her cheeks and looked across at Sag Harbor.

The water was choppy both coming and going.

She lifted her voice and called out to the sea
"I am going to sell this house and leave.
I'll come back someday, but not to live here again.
I am going to Ireland and find my mother's story, learn what pushed her to give me up.

I will find any family I still have.
I am going to find myself and call me by my real name.
Amen."

Two letters in the attic, left undiscovered on Christmas

From Margaret Lynch, grandmother to Norah, Marian and Cara, to her sister
Mae in Vermont

21 July.1926

Dear Mae,

In hopes this letter comes to you before you leave for home. The country air should do you great good and ease your breathing, sister. We're all glad we sent you for these July weeks. Without cable or telephone there, I must write sad news.

Mae, our beautiful boy Vincent died today. Johnny put him in the little blue suit you sent him and tucked him in his carriage just outside the kitchen door. It was a warm morning and we knew the sun would be good for him. I baked a pie— apple—and when I set it on the window sill to cool, I stepped out, apron still on to jiggle Vin's carriage a bit.

Mae, I thought he was sound asleep, but no, he was cool and dead. He died. He was 6 months and 3 days old. He wasn't sick a bit, Mae.

I could still smell the hot apples.

God, what am I to do? Johnny's beside himself in grief and we are two lost souls here. When the first baby died, I thought I'd never love another baby, never feel that horrible pain of losing a baby again. And here I am.

Johnny and I just look at each other and cry and move from room to room.

People come over but I feel better alone. I want to sit here and think of the sweet things I know about both my babies and then, I think I'll have it all set in my mind so I won't lose them again.

I know when I talk to you more tears and words will come. Just sit with me, sister, and hold me. That will help some.

No one knows what to say to me. It's all right. I've been this low before and God saw me through. God and Johnny and time. Silly, isn't it. That old saw about time? But it's true. It's just that all the time lies ahead and all I see is white space forever.

Come home soon.
Your loving sister,

Peggy

Margaret meets John Lynch: in blue ink, faded, on lined white paper...

My writing. 1927

I am writing this down for my children in case they ever want to know more about me.

His brother Chris was the big strong one, full of Irish malarkey and blazing blue eyes that looked down on you, well, like I don't know what, but Chris had his eye on Therese and brought her to the Irish dance of a Saturday night, dancing so well and sneaking sips of beer but not so's Therese would notice, she told me later, and it was this Chris, his brother Joe and even red-faced Tom who all piled into the open car one Sunday for a drive from Hell's Kitchen all the way here to Jamaica where, Chris told them, this grand lot of Irish girls lived in one house watched over by their big bosomed mother, the Irish mam of the lot leaning over the front porch with one eye to the street and the other cast over her girls who were as good as anyone could hope, especially her tall dark eyed Peg, the beauty of them all my dad said and didn't she have more polish to her than some as were putting on airs down the street like those Italian people; I was in my white shirtwaist standing bold as you like right next to my mother, on the porch, on that June Sunday when I put my hands over my eyes against the sun and saw big Christy driving and the older, smaller, milder looking brother Johnny sitting right next to him, his college sweater whiter than my dress even, and that dress was the best one I ever sewed. That is the way I remember seeing Johnny for the first time.

16 Fly Away

On January 20, Marian walked through Times Square, collar up against the wind, letting the sounds and honking cabs float around her. She remembered being a little girl, holding her aunt's hand rushing up a street and asking if they "were in a parade?" She smiled at the memory and once again felt she was in a parade, the energy of New York pushing her along. On her way to the Schubert Theater to get tickets for Cara and herself to see **Spamalot**, she realized a really large crowd was gazing up at the huge screen. There was Barack Obama, one hand raised, one on the Bible, swearing with all his young confidence to "save and protect the constitution of the United States, so help me God." Tears came to Marian's eyes and she sent him her love and hope. He was new in every single way possible and looked like hope. Her mind went back for a second to Georgeanne Evans. "She must be ecstatic today."

Tickets in hand, she slipped into a small Italian restaurant on 44th Street, one she had visited before. In a corner booth, she sipped a glass of good Chianti and made notes. Her plans were forming more clearly now.

The weeks in New York with Cara had opened her eyes to the beautiful and exhausting life of a dancer. Rehearsals, classes, stretching, nursing twisted muscles. Staying healthy and ready for the work, whatever the next role would be.

Cara had resumed work part time with the Martha Graham Company, teaching their newest recruits in the academy attached to the main studio. Her students were in Level 1 and were learning the basics. While some had hopes to advance to the main company, some simply were exploring. Graham work was in the winter intensive and, not ready to teach solo at that strenuous level, she went to class as often as she could and monitored progress with Miki, the main instructor.

The days fell into a pattern of morning exercise, walk and subway to the school, classes, light lunch, take class when possible, home, dinner and sleep. The very daily routine of it soothed Cara, and Marian had wisely just let her be.

In a while, Cara should get the grant decision, due out May 1. What then? Cara needed new life and direction and Marian knew in her gut that she did too and had to get on with...something. She left the restaurant and walked cross town to the river. Going down 42nd St she paused to muffle up even more and out of the corner of her eye, saw a small brown bird flailing at the window inside a closed bank. It kept throwing itself with crazy abandon at the window, trying to get out. But the bank was locked and no one seemed to notice, or care. Marian looked around helplessly, trying to think of a way to release the tiny bird. She couldn't. She regarded the doomed creature sadly, and walked on to the Hudson. Once on the pier, she found a table at the very end, away from tourists, away from everything but the water.

The river, gray and churning in winter air, slapped at the piers and flowed south to the Atlantic and beyond. It just went away unconcerned about Marian or Paul, unconcerned about her future or that of the trapped bird. It just went away, somewhere.

The college needs answers about me. Am I going back next semester? Emails from Sister William had been getting more insistent. No, I am not going back there. I am going on ahead someplace new. It is time to be frightened again, to taste uncertainty and stretch beyond what I think remotely possible.

Our honeymoon in Costa Rica had been like that. And this spring, before the rainy season, we were going back. That might have changed everything. The tickets were paid for, two to San Jose in April. She would go. Cara would not get results about the application until May 1, so maybe she could come along. It was a path.

A big labrador sprang out of nowhere, slobbering for a Frisbee in the air. Clear -eyed focus, a high jump and the dog had her prize. Another problem was Nelly. What to do. She can't be boarded forever and all these new roads and choices didn't seem to include a dog. She loved this animal fiercely. How could she let her go? But I think I have to. Maybe the ranch will take her on. She's so lovable with new dogs that she could be a mom to lonely visitors. Worth a try. An almost forever decision. Patty knew Nelly well and her polite e-mails seemed to have a layer underneath them. Like, what's with you and your dog, lady? I'm not an animal shelter.

She would see. Here, now, it felt good just to watch a beautiful dog jump for joy.

Later that night she broached the idea of Costa Rica to Cara. "Gee, I don't know, Marian. Graham is waiting for me to be really healed. I don't really have a job, things are so slow for me and the grant is looming large…..yeah, Costa Rica sounds pretty much like heaven! You sure?"

Maps came out, websites poured forth information and Marian found the EcoArts tour she was booked for. We would start in San Jose, travel by SUV to the rain forests to the north and then end by crossing the country to the Pacific side seeing more tropical changes.

"Paul and I stayed at Casa Esperanza on our honeymoon and we were finally going back." She was quiet. "It's OK. Part of me is there and I need to find it again. " She grinned broadly. "And I love the idea of being the experienced lady in the jungle to show you around."

17 Puzzles

Jigsaw puzzles have a rhythm of their own. You have to start with the border, naturally, and then eye promising chunks. Some puzzles tempt with bright colors or a particular hill or building. That can be the first bit and work out from there. One daunting puzzle of a Durer print of a rabbit is a study in browns, greys, and cream. You can work around the rabbit's outline. Durer's brush marked the tiniest of fur tufts, single whiskers and small hairs raised up on the ears, the wonderful long ears. It takes a long time, but eventually even the cream background falls into place rather quickly. But that is near the end. You have to work very hard to get all the pieces ready to go.

It was like that for two months, until by the end of March some significant pieces were lined up. Norah finished up with the house sale, which had occurred swiftly, turned her beloved Seamus over to her neighbor, finally cleared out and flew to Ireland. She had been remarkably still about whatever was happening there, but Marian and Cara decided she was finding a place to stay, plan her reconnaissance tours, make contacts and get set up with a computer, too. They really had no way to reach her and so, they waited and wondered.

Cara completed a six week stint of intermediate dance classes at the center and began hunting for tropical hiking gear. UPF shirts and pants, thick socks with wicking, hats, binoculars, bug spray and a whole raft of items prescribed by EcoArts. Marian footed the bill. "I'll gear you up and get you there. Then all the meals and shopping can be your bill. It's ok."

"Well, can I have a pony, too?"

"Smartass. I can't wait to see you all dressed for attack."

Once the two of them finished shopping and tried all the stuff on, they looked like they could find Dr. Livingston in the Congo. No animal of any kind was going to invade their pants, shoes, or shirts. They were good to go.

And go they did. For two April weeks, they would visit a mountain lodge with hikes above the cloud forest and trek through lowland jungles near the west coast of Costa Rica. In the deep, consuming quiet, immersed in many shades of green, they would find buried treasure.

Before the trip started, Marian went back to Los Angeles to discuss her situation with the President, Sister William, on campus. The religious asked some probing questions.

"Are you escaping or on a journey? We so treasure you here. Open your heart to the many paths of a journey to something good and you will find the way. Keep in touch—I will always care about you. And Nelly. I hear Costa Rican beer is wonderful. Enjoy it all. And maybe come back! " A leave of absence was agreed upon amicably with more warm wishes that she return to Immaculate Heart College soon.

Nelly went berserk when she saw Marian. This was not easy, to love this sweet dog so much and know another goodbye was ahead. The dog stood up on her hind legs, put her paws on Marian's shoulders and looked her in the eyes.

Patti watched this from the barn.

"You are not here to take her back, are you?" in more of a statement than a question.

"No...I....I don't know what to say."

"Well, you were right about her being a mama to the visitors. She just loves them all up. I'll keep her until you really know what you are about. How's that?" Her face smiled and so did her heartfelt voice.

"You are a good woman Patti. How can I thank you?"

"You just keep looking and when you are ready, Curt and I will send this pup home to you, wherever you wind up." She choked up then.

Marian stayed a few hours with her dog and when she had to go she explained in a soft voice that she would be back.

Nelly burrowed her big black face into Marian's arms and nosed her all the way up to her head. Then the dog went off, slowly. She knew.

The Three Graces: Costa Rica

The visitor is warned not to touch any tree bark as toxins may invade the skin. Walk extremely carefully aware of snakes and insects on the forest floor.

---Costa Rica GuideBook

18 Pura Vida

As the plane moved through the night, Marian reviewed her paperwork again.   The tour Marian and husband bought last year included the Hotel Quetzal at the start and end of the trip with two remote lodges in between. Not a honeymoon this time, Marian thought, but certainly a time to think, to be. And nice to have a friend along, her newfound cousin. Cara was beautiful, petite, powerful, and funny. She wanted to know her better. This trip had built- in quiet, private times, so they would not need to talk constantly or try to amuse each other. That had been appealing to Cara, she knew.

A few hours later, driving from the San Juan airport with warm breezes blowing into the cab, Marian looked out at the tin roofed shacks glinting in moonlight in the industrial section. Spanish voices and laughter drifted from open doors and the cab careened up dark hills, twisty roads, around corners and there stood the hotel, light on, Spanish tiled roof and courtyard. The white stucco gleamed and an attendant waved her in.

"Welcome, Señora, we are now expecting you to be here. Please come in."

The lobby and adjacent rooms were comfortably sized, decorated in cool greens and yellows and presented a not -so-foreign ambiance. She could have been in Florida or Hawaii. But her memories were awakening and she knew the true pura vida was beyond the city.

Too tired to think any more, Marian found her room, sank into a soft bed and slept. Jasmine and angel tree scents mingled with raucous bird song to waken her mid-morning. She remembered learning that the seductive white trumpet shaped blooms lured bats into them, releasing the black creatures at night. Beware! Beyond the open window, the mountains of Costa Rica stood elegant and removed.

At a breakfast of mango, pineapple, papaya, wonderful coffee and soft rolls, Marian looked up to see Cara walking toward her, a broad smile lighting her face.

"We made it!" Cara sat down and helped herself to coffee. "Our adventure begins!"

"I feel like an anxious travel agent," Marian confessed. "I really wanted everything to go just right."

"Well, it did, thank you. Just a little Texas delay between flights. I think I got in just after you last night. " Cara looked around in appreciation. Marian interjected "I was thinking that today may be our only day to see the city, so we can take a cab in and walk just about everywhere. It will be mountains and forests and jungle after today."

And so they zipped around San Jose, seeing the aging cathedral, spending time in the art museum, hunting for craft treasures in the Marketa Central and lunching at a small restaurant trying to decipher the posted menu. They loved the casados blending chicken and rice, and fried plantain and had a few gallos, open- faced tacos.

Dawn found the cousins grabbing a quick meal with luscious fresh fruit before boarding a well-appointed small van with room for 10 but holding only 6 for the journey. A German couple talked earnestly much of the way in German with enthusiastic nods to Marian and Cara. Two men from Canada seemed the most promising companions, yet they signaled a need for privacy.

"Perfect," sighed Marian. "I was terrified we'd wind up in a noisy bunch of tourists wanting noise and constant talking. This should be nice and quiet."

Totally, signaled Cara, both thumbs up.

The four-hour journey climbed higher and ever higher up the Talamanca Mountain range, passing the Cerro de la Muerte, passing the cloud level.

"I'm not in Kansas, Toto. I feel like we are going to heaven. What can be higher than this?" Cara was glued to the window.

Looking down on a misty sea of clouds, the women thought about what was ahead, while letting their overworked minds deconstruct themselves, allowing stray thoughts to arise and depart, abandoning unfruitful threads, stepping down to this moment, now.

La Casa Esperanza was reached by a narrow and perilous road that brooked no traffic complications. One vehicle and that was it. A small car backed down to a cutback area and allowed the van access. They turned down a winding path surrounded by dense foliage and high, overarching trees and then the driver pulled over.

"Here, you must look down for this is the valley you will be in. Now you can see where you will be for five nights." Pride in this place was in his eyes.

"¿Es magñifico, no?" Jose gestured to the valley grandly.

"Oh yes, sí!" exclaimed Marian and Cara in unison.

Green. Light green, dark fern green, yellow green, blue green.

Trees lifting and swaying in strong breeze. Trees so dense no light separates them.

Flowers. Pink and red bougainvillea, improbable yellow iris, orchids, and more whose names were to be discovered.

And humming above it all, birds. Yellow, green, some with red hatch marks, black with red wings, hawks...more with yet unknown names sweeping and soaring, playing in the air.

In the midst of ponds and archways lay a lodge of modest extensions. Tucked into the hills were small cottages following paths into the rain forest.

All was still, very, very quiet.

A hawk circled above the valley.

"¿Todo esta bién, señoras?"

"Sí! Oh yes, sí!"

19 New Paths

Life settled into a comfortable pattern here at Casa Esperanza. Breakfast was prepared and waiting every morning. Helpful young cooks prepared omelets. Many kinds of fruits, ready for breakfast, worked their way into crushed fruit drinks later in the day or toppings for desserts.

Fresh fish from the trout stream and more from the rivers. Vegetables grown on the site. Tender Costa Rican beef, grass fed. Chickens that ranged free and produced perfect eggs.

Not a place for dancing and noise, Casa encouraged eco tourism and centered visitors.

Cara and Marian found themselves talking at breakfast, taking long walks on the marked trails, resting or writing or painting after lunch and finding each other at dinner. It was peaceful, restorative and full for each woman. They found that they were coming to love each other in a new family kind of way and that they respected each other's time and space. Neither felt anxious with the other.

Cara thought to herself on one of those walks ,"I want to remember it all. You get to La Casa Esperanza after hours of driving up windy mountain roads. Leaving San Jose, you see fields, small houses with tin roofs, men walking slowly along village roads. Children stop and stare at you as you pass. Then only dense mountain green, ferns arching for light, vines hugging the hillsides, and clouds. You go above the clouds but you are not flying either on your own bird wings or in an airplane. Soft grey puffs, the clouds hang like a pewter necklace around the massive hills and all that is beneath them disappears, is no more.

The lodge is tucked into a deep valley with hills and forests all around. It is silent. People walk gently and quietly, even as they work. Everyone is here for a special reason—for some, it is the birds, hundreds of them flying at dawn before the heat sets them down. Others come to walk the forest trails, going farther every day. That seems to be the mission of the fellow travellers who were in our bus. Never see them.

Why am I here?

You need to go out and touch this country in some way every day and then return here for fresh fish and vegetables at every meal. Life slows down and your breath comes in different, smooth patterns. There is no television or radio and phone only sometimes.

You listen to your heart beat. You breathe through your heart; your breath goes in and out slowly. And you think. Not in an aggressive "to do list" sort of way, but in discursive ways that raise your memories and you see them drift by along with your hopes, your fears, your vision of hummingbirds coaxing nectar from a feeder, the smell of flowers all around. You have no choice but to deeply meditate. Martha Graham knew this. "It all begins with the breath," she said.

I walked into the forest with a guide one morning, listening to new rules. In New York, I can start to cross before the light, leaving tourists behind, wobbling for safety. I can catch a subway in a flash and choose other routes if one is closed. I know where the best street carts are for lunch and I sit on my favorite bench just inside Central Park.

I know my way around.

Here, I must not touch anything. Anything. The bark of the tree I latch onto for secure footing as I climb may be poisonous. The ants beneath my feet are on a cutting mission, carrying leaves to a nest miles away. I must not step on them. I need to look up, not just down at my feet. I have to stop and be still to let the morning sun and shadows filter through the moist, thick foliage and look up lest I miss a monkey floating across to a better tree. The bromeliads grow on bare bark and make their own horizontal root system, since they can't get ground soil. They are wonderful in purples, reds and oranges.

I am learning the rules and breathing thin air."

20 The Snake as an Agent of Change

On the sixth day, their last one at Casa Esperanza, deep in the forest, as they stood marveling at the cutter ants working like demons to get one special leaf to take back to their nests, Marian began to cry. Cara just held her a bit and said nothing. They were alone in the rain forest. Far off, monkeys screeched in the trees and a large agouti crept across their path.

"What's all this, then? " crooned Cara.

"I want to start all over. All, all over. I've been living like these goddamned ants, trying to get the right fucking leaf and cram it into the hole and then marching right out to get another damned leaf. And half the time when I haul it back to the nest, some fucking quality control ant supervisor tells me it did not make the cut!"

They laughed, then, and stared down at the scurrying ants. Stepping over the mile long line of the busy creatures, the two women walked on, talking softly.

"We can't sit down because we might harm some tree surface or invite some poisonous bug into our shirts. We can't touch anything. So, we keep moving. It seems like my life has been like that for too long. Something dangerous may get me and I better get going."

Cara touched Marian's back and felt sweat through her shirt. She sensed her own sweat running between her breasts.

"Look—" She pointed up.

Ahead of them on the trail, the breath of fog in the forest hovered over a thicket so green it was black. Rustling sounds spoke for unseen lizards, moles, snakes writhing around airborne roots and bromeliads.

Above, a second tier of purple flowers hung thick, with muscular vines seeking light, a provenance.

Cara whispered. "2:00 o'clock, right, long branch curving right. Just before the sunlight."

There they were. Two Resplendent Quetzals. Regal, serenely uninterested in all above and below them, their extravagant tails filled the emptiness beneath the horizontal branch with red, purple, and blues. The birds took in the day, unperturbed, and if they were aware of people beneath them, they gave no sign.

Hot air pressed Marian's neck and chest. Anxious ants forgotten, she seemed to rise from her sweating body and become a quetzal herself. With them she could be in amongst her doubts, her uncertainties, and rise above them all with contemplative dignity.

They had an answer she needed.

In the highlands, rain pours straight down sending birds scurrying, flattening grasses, swirling the green clay rocks into turquoise mud.

Across the Rio Savegre, cows lie down by the rushing water, enjoying surcease while the white horse leans to eat the wet young grass.

Back at Casa, over glasses of cold white wine, Marian tried to make sense of the day.

"When we got back today, I reached for the doorknob and saw a thin green line at the door. It was a snake. I almost missed it. He settled right into the doorframe. When I moved a little, he went off like a shot. I looked where he went and saw nothing until I saw an eye looking back at me. This was an iguana, frozen in high grass with one eye keeping me at bay. He looked like a medieval knight in heavy armor. I just looked back and finally he shifted his huge body around and the other eye looked away.

A steward from our inn came over and pointed out another snake, one very deadly, the fer-de-lance. It, too, was magnificent. Had it bitten me, blood would pour from my eyes and quite probably I would die. With a hatchet, he killed it in one swoop.

Now the moral of this story is that I was not a real threat to any of those guys and I blest them unaware. Do you remember that line from 'Rime of the Ancient Mariner?' The sailor had killed an albatross for no reason. It was just there. And he killed it. He is cursed and doomed until he looks into the black ocean one night and sees slimy sea creatures. Actually, he thinks they are iridescent and beautiful. The spell is broken and he is back in nature's arms.

I think I broke my curse today."

"What curse?"

"The one where no one can touch you. The one where you don't even see animals and you just check for the weather to know what to wear. The one where you will probably lose or at least get hurt. The one where beautiful quetzals arrange themselves in trees like kings and queens and you never see them. The one where everyone dies."

Cara was at a loss. What was the root of this? She decided to take a radical turn.

"Marian, tell me about your mother. I wonder if she was anything like mine. If you could talk to her now, what would you ask? "

"I would ask my mother about death, about loss. I want to know how she kept breathing and when she could stop reminding herself to breathe. When she wasn't numb and wrapped in thick cotton swaddling any more. Did she ever love someone fiercely and lose him? Was that Tim, the one in her letters to your mom? Or was she afraid to love, did she hold back? Would Tim have changed everything for her? Because I can't see my past very well and I know I have to change in some major ways.   I've been very tidy and organized and one damn step just followed the last and I don't know where it got me except to this jungle with steaming plants, standing stock still while monkeys scream.

I study art. I teach college students how to see art. That is what I do, but not who I am. I am all alone and my husband is dead. This is not a normal vacation. Why am I here?"

Cara said nothing for a few minutes. Finally, she said this to her cousin:" Now look at those monkeys picking at each other. They preen and smooth each other's fur, picking out juicy bugs as treats, no judgment, and no critical eye, just sitting very close and helping each other out.

Why did my mother hide and run away? What frightened her so? Did she love me too much, not enough, not understand how she could have created a freak like her? Was I the monkey that needed to be left out on the limb, shivering alone? Was she so mortified, so ashamed of herself? Whatever. She was gutless and she damn well should have smiled at me and told me I was wonderful.

Because I am."

21 River Stones

They left Casa Esperanza regretfully, hoping to remember it forever. The beautiful hostess, Maritza, bid them a kind farewell, urging they return some day. The small bus took them to the Pacific Coast after traveling for some hours stopping near Playa Hermosa in a tiny circle of cottages called La Casa de Maria. Some nuns had lived there years ago but had since moved on to other missions. Their small chapel remained standing.

On their next to last day in Costa Rica, Cara and Marian ventured out on their last rainforest walk. The path curved lower and lower, pulling Marian and Cara down to the sound of rushing water. The river cascaded into a series of waterfalls, releasing sprays of misty water as it clambered to the next level. Columns of solid white water like Greek temple columns poured in liquid surges, never stopping, never changing. At the base of the falls, large flattened rocks pushed into the middle of the now placid stream.

Cara called a halt. "Let's stop here. I have an idea for the dance, if I get the grant, and I want to make some notes. And we can eat our sandwiches, too." Thirsty, they gulped down cold water, munched on chicken sandwiches and gazed into the water, stupefied.

Cara made a few pages of notes and sketches. Still looking into the blue-grey water, Cara asked quietly, "Will you really tell me about Paul now?"
    Marian began:

"When I first saw Paul, he was in a corner at a large party, with people all around him. He was the one talking. I don't know even now what he was saying, but those people couldn't get enough of him. He laughed, his arms flapped around, and everyone was right there with him.
    He was 20.
    I couldn't get enough of him either. He was beautiful. Dark skin, black hair in a slick crew cut that looked wet. A tight white tee shirt over jeans. My date saw me staring at him and poor Jim knew he was done.
    "Who is that?" I asked in what sounded like a pretty non-committal tone to me.

"That's Paul Driscoll. Kind of full of himself. Let's dance..."

"Anyway, that was how we met." Marian fell silent and as the waters churned around her, she went back to that party, September 29, 1978, remembering...

....

Jim wandered off in search of a beer and Marian wound her way back to where she had seen Paul. He was gone. Before she could turn around, there he was.

"Hi, I'm Paul Driscoll. I haven't seen you before."

I looked into those dark eyes and got lost. I must have said something. Next minute, we were dancing to a slow number and I felt Paul hold me for the first time. We talked later, but we knew we had to get out of there. I left old Jim and we drove into the California night, taking the coast toward Malibu.

September is hot in Los Angeles and the warm breezes softly wrapped me.

"I think I need to see you pretty much every day from now on," Paul announced as the night enveloped us.

"I know. That's right." Paul smiled but he could not see the full smile on my face. It was too dark. And that was it.

When he dropped me off at my apartment in Santa Monica, I turned into his arms and night breezes pulled us together, the moon stopped for just a second, and that kiss, our first, would never be matched again. We would live on that kiss for 20 years."

"That sounds perfect, " Cara offered.

"Well, it was. It was after we were married that the losses crept in.
We had to ask doctors then for pregnancy results then. It was agonizing every time. Every time I thought this one was the baby I would hold. And every time, it left. Paul was tender and sad. The sadness set in pretty hard and never seemed to lift after that April. I had stopped teaching in hopes of a successful pregnancy, and when I lost the third baby, I just stopped. Stayed home. Made a great garden. Took classes in photography, Italian cooking, anything to keep busy and not think. "

She put her water bottle down with a surprised look.

"That never really changed. I don't think we ever found each other again. Two was just not enough. A life stretching out ahead with no one else in it was our reality, and we were both frightened. We turned away from each other and into our own even smaller worlds. I think I just realized that right now. So then I became one of those leaf cutter ants scurrying to and fro in a semblance of important business. " She looked into the deepening purple twilight, the darkening rain forest receding from view.

"When we booked this trip, I think we both hoped to find our magic again and stop living politely parallel lives. At least I was. Now, I'll never know."

Cara sat silent, sharing the memories and the darkening skies. When she spoke, she was looking into the dark forest, not at Marian.

"I think you are in a great spot now. You were ready to find a new way, a happier life and leave the past behind. You still have that chance. You just don't see yet what is coming, but 'readiness is all.' That was Hamlet. I've been thinking about him, funny here of all places, but I always loved that play. He thought too damn much and dithered about what to do next for way too long. He wanted it all to be perfectly lined up and life doesn't serve that way.

I love him most when he finally relaxes and decides to let things take their own course. 'If it is to be now, 'tis not to come; if it be not now, yet it will come. Readiness is all.'

So, let it be. Buddhist, really, to let the river wash over the stone and you are the stone. The river won't erase you, but it will change you in subtle, permanent ways. Just be in the river for now."

Cara gazed at Marian's face.

"I've had time to think about things like this a lot the last few years. I want to tell you why, but not now. Now, we need to get back to the lodge, have our last dinner and a good sleep."

"Thank you, Cara, thank you. I'm lucky to have you."

"You had me at hello. Let's keep walking."

22 Departure

On this last late afternoon walk in the forest near Casa de Maria, before their departure early in the morning, Marian and Cara tried to look even more closely at the leaves, the birds, the ants, the roots before they would leave. Now they knew the wood creeper, the great egret, mango swallows, plovers, willets, purple gallineau, mot mots because they had seen them in the hills and swamps.

The steam of early morning mist joining heat rose around them even as shady spots retained chill. It felt like a cathedral, and arching trees demanding sunlight formed the apse, the vaulted ceilings. No stained glass needed here as light streamed into open spaces, flicking green into yellow, warming leaves to lie flat, veins exposed like leaded panes.

Without preamble, Cara walked ahead of Marian on a narrow bit, letting her question float behind her.

"Want to do something scary?"

"Define scary."

"Where you are so afraid you can't breathe."

"And you ask this now because........."

"Because there is a canopy walk ahead and no other choice but to walk over the trees."

Marian was seriously afraid of heights.

"I can't."

"You have to. And I will walk ahead of you and talk to you every step. And you don't have to look down. Plus we are really lucky because no one else is here to shake the ropes."

"The walkway moves?" This said in deep fear.

"Just a little."

Marian took a deep breath and started across and then retreated.

"I just can't."

"Yes you can."

She started again with Cara right in front of her talking all the way. She had no idea what Cara was saying, but she kept on going. It was not so bad, but she did not look down.

About halfway across, Cara stopped.

"What's the matter?" Marian asked, assuming disaster lurked, maybe an attack of monkeys.

"Absolutely nothing. This is a perfect place and a perfect moment. Don't think. Look and smell and breathe it all in."

Marian looked down, down into a deep ravine with vines consuming trees, each competing for sunlight, orchids cascading in impossible places and patterns, and she heard birds. Howler monkeys screaming in the distance.

Different birds calling, singing, talking to one another.

All fear left her.

She was standing where she could stand and the experience was whole and somehow, she knew nothing would ever be the same. She had faced this fear and could face more.

They completed the canopy walk with Marian feeling as if she had climbed an alp. Pride and joy filled her all the way up and Cara smiled, knowing.

The path was wide enough for two. And easier, now going downhill. Out of nowhere, Cara asked, 'so what happened when Paul died?"

Here it was. The elephant in the forest. The story she had not touched with anyone. Anyone.

Marian summoned up all the crushing images of that final day and gave a fairly full outline of events. The goodbye. The plan to meet in Carmel. The missed messages. The call to go to Madera and see a bloody body still in the blue windbreaker.

Cara listened to the sad chronicle and absorbed the implications of the surprising connection Marian had found in Madera. She now saw the core problem, the heart of darkness.

Slowly, she stated in a flat voice" So you think he had a double life."

"In a way, but not the way you'd think. It's that large chunks were separate from me. My office. His office. Longer days. More important cases. And where did I go then? Why didn't I chase all the way after him?"

"You told me about not having children. Was that too much to live with?"

"God, yes, at first. It just never happened and we moved on. Not consciously. It was sort of a drift. Maybe that's when I needed to stay even closer to him, but we moved apart. We reminded each other of what had not worked."

The women walked on through the humid forest, silent now.

Marian thought.

One night Paul came home from a trial, pretty late. I'd been researching an article for a journal and my deadline was crunching in. I had books everywhere, even in the kitchen. But I'd fixed a really good spaghetti sauce and dinner was ready.

He came in and got a beer from the fridge, popped it and took the top drink from it. He looked around the kitchen and just as I started to clear some books away, he stopped me with

"No, don't bother. It's ok. I'll just take a plate to my study."

Now that's not such a big deal, but he kept doing it through that trial, and more.

And more sorts of small things. "How was your day?" didn't provoke a long conversation asking for details. We'd both be tired and it came down to "Good. How about you?"

I can't remember the last time we flat out laughed with each other and had real fun. It was a while ago, maybe when we were in Spain.

That was one great thing we did together. We traveled well together. Being far away always made it easier to depend on each other, just be together.

In Madrid one night we walked for miles trying to find Hemingway's favorite restaurant. It was winter. We got lost but we were freezing and laughing at the same time. I looked up and saw white bits in the air and my California eyes thought maybe a fire was nearby. It was snowing and we stood in the Plaza Mayor in each other's arms, letting it fall all over us. We found the restaurant and ate and drank lots of red wine. Then we went back to the hotel and made love.

It was a perfect day.

On the other hand, January of 2006 was not perfect. Paul had been diagnosed with prostate cancer, a surprise at his age of 52. Prostate cancer. The "good one," but still—cancer. He didn't even tell me himself, not wanting to frighten me. If he was private, this was the far corner of his privacy.

The phone rang just as Oprah said, "You know, life can change in the time it takes to put on lipstick." So that puts it at about 3:35. Her show airs in Los Angeles from 3:00-4:00 pm and I'd watch if she didn't have truly bizarre people on or serial killers. "So, how did you **feel** after the 10th murder?" I forget who was on that day, but I picked up the phone just when she went to break.

"I am the oncologist at City of Hope," he said "and I need to talk to your husband." No shit.

So do I, I thought in a panic. I tried to talk, told him to call the office right away, now, please. It sounds important, I offered hollowly, needlessly. I had to force myself to breathe.

Now, Paul wouldn't let me tell anyone. He said he loved me and it was no big deal. An annoyance, really. His secret grew too large for our house.

I needed to tell someone and I did. I told people he would never see or meet. I told women I trusted. But I found myself turning down dinner invitations because I'd have to lie by omission.

We're fine.

It's all good.

Same old same old.

The actual surgery day went smoothly and I was alone with my thoughts during the 3-½ hour surgery. Apple blossoms floated down to the ground as I watched them drift from the waiting room window. Surgery called three times during the procedure, a kindness I had not expected. And so finally, the cancer was removed and Paul drifted into a drugged sleep most of the day.

I drove us home the next day with him singing his favorite Frank Sinatra songs with the radio and I knew I would do anything for him. Anything.

The weeks of recovery were actually a close time for us. I changed dressings, got him food, and checked on him often. Monitored visitors. We worked a jigsaw together. It was quiet. It was nice.

Marian resumed talking to Cara.

"So when Paul died, I had already made up my mind to truly handle this all alone. No mournful secretary crying, whining in her thin, pale voice. No. She would be needed for office transfers to the partners, but no more. Looking back on the day he died, before I knew I was a widow, I remember the sweet breeze sliding on my arms, the sun warming me through the canyon from the coast, and singing along to 'Hotel California' on the radio."

Just around the bend in the jungle, the river rose higher and a tree limb had fallen across the water, pointing deeper yet into green blackness. Walking carefully across the rushing river, Cara and Marian sucked in their breath and stepped tentatively. Above them, haze drifted over the high, bending trees. Grey afternoon light forced yellow to live on its own and all the greens to rise on the heat. A cow lay in the shade on the other side of the river.

Marian roused herself from the flitting memories and in a calm voice described to Cara the actual day of seeing Paul laid out in the morgue.

"I remember being led into a narrow white room. Paul was on a table, sheets folded around him. The doctor left me alone for a while. I don't know how long that was. He didn't have a mark on his face. He was the same handsome man who kissed me two mornings ago in that last eternity. I didn't touch him. I dreaded the cold skin. This was the man I knew I would die for. I hadn't been asked to, but when I cared for him after the cancer surgery, it was a wonderful surprise to feel that I still would do anything, anything for him. Whether he asked or not. Anything.

I didn't look at the crushed middle of him. So I left with a beautiful face to hold onto."

Clay robins darted through the trees. Black-cheeked woodpeckers drilled into obdurate wood. In a showy flash, a scarlet rumped tanager dashed through faltering light and was gone.

Wiping the sweat from her neck, Cara spoke quietly.

"Well, I'm no expert here, but it sounds like you both did all the right things. If you slipped away from each other, I really think this trip together would have given you time to find each other again. Just like when you were so close after the surgery.

That's not to say that this was a huge opportunity here that you missed. Neither one of you was lost. You were like these damn leaf cutter ants we keep hopping over. Each one of you was packing your leaf home on your back and you almost got there.

I'm sorry you only have me here, but I love you. And now that I have found you in the forest, I won't lose you."

Marian hugged Cara and turned up the gravel path to their adjoining rooms in a small cottage. By now it was dark.

Cara opened her door and then turned.
"Want a drink? The stars are huge tonight."

Wine glasses in hand they sat on their porch looking up at the Southern Cross embedded in the black night, silver shining over their valley.

That night they did not talk any more. Both women slept well. They each dreamed...

Marian's dream:

I know this beach. The rocks up ahead will break to another cove and I can walk into the water, see tide pools. The water is so warm. It never is warm here. Why is it warm now? Carmel---that's where I am –it's Carmel---water is freezing up here. But this water is warm. I don't want to get out.

Nelly!! There is Nelly swimming towards me! She is coming to get me.

I am on her back and we race over the top of the water! I am laughing and hugging her wet, black coat. I am not afraid and she even barks at the waves. We are deeper and deeper.

I fall off Nelly's back and she waves to me. Now I look down into the warm, sparkling water and the bright blue fish encircle me, nibble at my fingers and toes. They have pig faces. One has hot pink stripes and one has blue lines all over and eyes on only one side.

Nelly dives to get me and we swim to shore.

What street is this? Where is my house? We walk and walk. Twisted black green pine trees bend down to grab me and Nelly runs away. She is gone. I can't find her or the house.

I see it now and the seashells at the door and I have a key but it won't go in.

I hear Paul. I know he's in there. I claw at the door and my hands bleed bleed bleed.

Sweating, Marian woke up.

That same night, Cara dreamt, too.

I'm onstage. It's a performance night. The audience is out there in the dark. I can feel the waves of excitement through the blue velvet curtain. I hear my measure, have my count and I'm out, long full skirt whipping around my legs, my bare feet. The wood is cool.

I turn to find my partner, but he's not there. I try not to panic but I can't move; I'm frozen. The audience is murmuring in unsettled sounds. They sound like bees.

I can't move.

Then, I look offstage and all the dancers turn away and go home. Except me. My partner waited until they all left. Now the audience gets up all at once and they are laughing; they've forgotten I am there and they go.

The theater is dark but at the waterfall in the middle of the room, yellow birds fly all around, beating their wings furiously. A green parrot glides past and ten toucans perch on their tree, ruffle their feathers and peer at me.

My partner and I dance into the waterfall and birds light on our shoulders---plovers, a swallow-tailed kite, a magnificent frigate and ten resplendent quetzals, a spoonbill. I laugh and look at the other dancer moving in gradual sweeps, rising to take me in her arms. It is Keiko.

23 Fall Only to Rise: Cara

Brian Gallagher was this boy in my government class senior year. He had red hair, joked a lot, played basketball, and we were sort of buddies, I guess. He sat next to me 3 periods a day. Brian would tap his heel very softly pretty much all the time and I kidded him about that.

Well, I didn't know what to say when he asked me to prom. Hadn't a clue THAT would happen. He looked like a scared puppy when he asked me and I just said, "Sure. That's great."

Mom was the happiest I can remember when I told her. Her eyes set on something just next to my head and she started planning.

"We'll get the dress in the city. We'll go in and get you a wonderful dress no one else will have. And a haircut in that fancy salon in the mall. Do you think you want your hair up? Up, that would be perfect."

She had turned into a prom machine. I had no say, actually, because I didn't want to disappoint her by telling her I really didn't want to go at all.

The night came, May 10th, and Brian brought me a gardenia and when we walked out to his dad's car, borrowed for the night, I looked back and saw Mom and Dad in the doorway, Mom in front. The living room lights were bright behind them. Dad's hand was up in a silent salute and Mom's smile and waving hand was full of hope, happy hope.

When I waved back, I knew I was living a lie and I was ready to leave that house of lies. I wanted to dance, all right, just not with boys. Mom died two years later. I'm glad I gave her that night.

Some nights I dream about that door and the backlit silhouettes, and I turn back as Brian melts away. I'm in my baby blue prom dress and I go to Mom and we go back inside and she just holds me and says, "I know, I know. You'll be fine."

Two years after graduation, I was taking class at Kansas State, studying dance and business, the business as a backup after my yet-to-be dancing career. My mother Kathleen died in her sleep one night in June 1993. I had no chance for a goodbye.

Unexpected, silent, just...gone. Funeral, cakes,
flowers, silence in the house, unanswered
questions hung in the air.
Dad, now a widower, worked steadily, cleaning out
things, clothes, busying himself in the garage doing,
most likely, nothing at all.

Shortly after Kathleen died, Dad came down to
breakfast one morning, an envelope in his hand.
Neither of us could cook much, so the meal was
cereal, toast, and coffee, just like every other day.

I eyed the envelope, but said nothing about it.

Dad placed it just next to his coffee spoon so the
blue line of the envelope's top flap was perfectly
parallel. He touched the envelope.

Into his second cup of coffee, he cleared his
throat.

"Lady." His pet name for me caught in his
throat and came out in a knot.

"Lady," he began again, "it's time for you to go to
New York. This money will get you started."

After a minute's silent pause, I reached for the
blue envelope, my hand grazing his.

"Dad, I thought I'd work in town at the studio a
bit more until you're.."

" 'Settled' ?" he cut in. "OK? That's where I am
now. Your mother was a good woman but she
never, ever, let herself go, be herself. She was
ashamed because she loved me, I know, and loved

you, too, but she never knew how to show it. There were some things we never talked bout. Never.

But she knew you would never get married to a man and it broke her heart to think you'd be as lonely as she was, deep down. Cara, I want you to fly away, dance in New York. And," here he took a long breath, "and if you find some girl you want to bring home to me, well then, I'm going to be happy as all get out to see her in this house. Listen to me, lady girl. There is nothing, nothing you could ever do to make me stop loving you. Nothing. So, you need to go now."

I remember looking into my dad's grey eyes and for the first time talked to him as his adult lesbian daughter, a woman fully poised to fly, to dance, to love.

    *   *

            *

Cara applied to audition for Juilliard in Chicago two months later, jumped up and down when she received her acceptance letter and left Thornton on Sept.1, 1999, five thousand dollars in her wallet, dance shoes, tights, her ticket to New York and the address of Juilliard.

New York City never frightened Cara. When the airport bus let her out at Port Authority on 42nd St, she got out onto the street breathing in hot pretzel smells, hearing long fire engine wails, jackhammers pounding away on some old building, feeling people rush in front of her, behind her, all in fast, purposeful strides while she looked east and west, chose west and came home to the city she had always known she'd love.

She found a cab, told her driver the address off 78th Street for Juilliard housing She drank in Broadway, twisting left and right to catch glimpses of buildings so high she couldn't see the top from the cab's back seat. A million cars, packed streets, glossy windows, food carts on corners, shops with antiques, dress boutiques with high fashion manikins in the windows. It was perfect and it certainly wasn't Thornton.

"What do I owe you," she asked the cabbie.

"Lookit the meter, lady. That's it."

"Oh. Right." She gave him the fare and a $2 tip.

She stepped out of the cab and looked at her first New York apartment with Kansas eyes. Inside the lobby, a friendly 6-foot tall doorman came over to welcome her with a smile.

"Well now, hello. You look to me like a brand new dancer. Would that be about right?" He chuckled, picked up Cara's heavy suitcase and gave her the key to 4F.

"Now, it's only this once I'll wait on you, see. You go on up. I'm Joe. Your other dancing lady is already there waiting."

Other? Waiting? Cara didn't know what to expect as the elevator rattled up to 4. Down a sideways twisting hallway she turned a corner and saw 4F, door wide open and jazz floating out into the hall.

Inside somewhere, the "other dancing lady" was on the phone, laughing.

"Gotta go. I think Joe just sent up my new roommate."

Long black hair streaming down her back, an elegant, petite Japanese woman turned to see Norah and her dark eyes took her in, a welcoming smile lighting her face.

"Are you Cara? Ted arranged the roommates and I think I am the lucky one. Welcome to Juilliard; I'm Keiko Ishikawa."

Her hand reached out to touch Norah's lightly and her lingering touch told Norah she was really welcome.

"Go unpack, wash up, whatever, and we can go to the rehearsal hall. I'm guessing you want to see the school right away, yes?"

Norah felt exhaustion cascade over her. All the energy that flew her to New York was slipping now, but she said—"Oh, gosh. Do you mind? I'm so curious to see it all."

"Sure. God knows you'll be there enough hours and months to love it and hate it, but that first look is pretty special."

Walking crosstown to Lincoln Center, Norah felt the winter cold seep into her bones but all she could hear was Keiko's soft voice relaying her own odyssey from Tokyo to New York and dance.

"My family has a small grocery store in Tokyo. I have two brothers and one sister and they're all in the family business one way or another. I couldn't do it. No way. I left Japan for New York 14 years ago. First I stayed with my cousin Yuriko in Soho and I started taking classes at a studio down there. I studied ballet and some modern in Tokyo but it was never what I really wanted.

My whole family thought I was nuts, well, for lots of reasons. One night the Alvin Ailey company performed in Tokyo on tour and after I saw them, I knew I had to throw out my ballet slippers, go barefoot on a wooden stage and move, move, into those great, deep swirls and stretches.

It took some doing but I didn't care how much they got it or didn't. I left. I had some money from my grandfather. Here we are. What do you think?"

Lincoln Center possesses Columbus Avenue from 62nd to 66th Street like a queen spreading her robes, waiting for all comers to touch her throne.

Facing the Metropolitan Opera with its high glass windows, the great chandelier shining out to the plaza, Cara could hardly breathe. She just nodded and drank it in full of awe.

What went on in there? What waves of word, music, passion? To her right, Avery Fisher Hall, and finally, the façade of Juilliard.

Keiko turned to Cara. "Welcome home. In you go. I'll introduce you to Brandon if he's around and show you our current rehearsal hall and get you your locker. "

Smells. Leather, sweat, sandwiches, dusty floors, sweat. Wonderful, wonderful smells. Dancers clipped by, erect, hair up, busy chatter following after them. One girl stretched out taping her toes so she could dance over and through the blisters. Loose pants covered long legs warming up. Soft, light scarves around sensitive necks. Leotards with stitches, holes, snags. Dancers propped up against walls watching their peers rehearse, looking for moves to steal, to copy. Sensing fear, anticipating falls. Thinking ahead to when they would dance the principal roles.
Cara turned from soaking all this in to see a tall, handsome man with friendly eyes, saying something to her.

"It's a lot to take in, right? I'm Brandon and we'll be working together a lot in Dance 101. Keiko will show you the ropes and get you a good dinner tonight, right, Keiko? Then see you in the morning. Good luck!" And Brandon Smith, first year Director of Dance, was off down the hall, sweater lightly folded around his neck.

Later, over slices of Ray's pizza and cold drinks, Keiko and Cara planned ahead.
"Sort of a goodbye to pizza for a while, so enjoy. We'll walk down 5th Avenue later and get some frozen yogurt and see the stores up close. Sound ok?"

That night was more than OK. Cara slipped into New York like a cat on a couch. She never looked back and owned the city from that night on.

24   Cara's Diary. 1999

September. I love it all. No time to write everything down! The new girls are so good—hope I can keep up. One guy has become a friend and we sort of support each other through pain and sweat. Max. Later.

October. Getting colder here now. It takes longer to warm up in the studio. Classes go well and are starting to kind of blur together. Keiko keeps me healthy and surprises me with great Japanese soups sometimes. She is beautiful inside and out.

November. We will dance a new piece and competition is fierce for positions. I work whenever I can and sneak in some extra time after hours. I love being alone in a semi-lit room, feeling the wood beneath me, arching, moving, stretching. I'm becoming numb to being watched. I just get into my zone and it doesn't matter who watches or what mistakes I make. I just go down my own road.

December. Dad is coming here for Christmas! He says it is just too dreary to try at home and so we will have a New York Christmas! Lights are up all over and I got free tickets for a few performances at Lincoln Center to show off my home to Dad. I miss him. Miss him.

January. OK flu is here in the big apple biiiiiig time. So gross. Many classes cancelled. Want to die.
Now.

March. I forget February. I do remember one great night, though. After nursing me back to health with strange and wonderful Japanese concoctions, Keiko looked at me carefully one night and just opened her arms, encircled me, and slipped into bed with me. Heaven came to earth. We found every nook and cranny, exploring, kissing, touching. Dancers are very agile, it turns out. And so I am finally and I hope forever, in love. I called Dad to tell him and he just laughed.

"Well, hell, I could see that! What took you so long?" What a guy.

April. Some audition panel is here from the Danse Italia Company in Tuscany. I am dancing with Keiko in Appalachian Spring and we've got it down as much as beginners can. Easy as a breath right now. Other days, I feel like a cow. It is as good as I can be for now so it will have to do. Being careful not to bruise, strain, sprain!!

May. This fairy tale is eerily wonderful. It can't be happening! I am in love with a wonderful gal (credits to South Pacific) and we, WE, we, are going to Italy for the summer! The day of the audition, two other duos backed out and it came down to Max, I do love that man, 3 seniors, and Keiko and me. I. We had asked to be considered together and it worked! In a segment from **Appalachian Spring**, we were sort of together and sort of not. The sequence occurs when the Pioneer Woman (me) dances solo with gestures to the Bride (Keiko). I am blessing her. I loved the Graham works and watched the old black and white video of Martha herself many times.

*   *

*

I stopped my journal when we left for Italy. Everything from that summer
glows in my mind with a deep Tuscan gold. I want to bring every second back, so writing this now is so important. If I don't get it all right I might lose it forever and I have already lost so much.

There were a dozen dancers there from various schools. We arrived over the course of two days, sleepy from long flights, a bus ride from Milan's Aerporto Malpensa to the villa in Lucca. Lucca is a medieval walled village of twisting paths, stone walls, crumbling fences, olive trees, hot, hot air and a view of the valley around. Looking out from the highest via you see green and gold fields squared off against each other, tidy vineyards, dusty roads and deep blue sky filled with enormous puffy white clouds. Sometimes it is too hot to breathe. When a breeze comes up in late afternoon, your skin drinks it in.

A rich benefactress, Marta de Artan, donated her villa every summer for dance academia. Her daughter was a dancer until she was crushed in a horse accident. The horse stumbled in the rough fields and not only fell on the girl but rolled over her legs several times. Mercifully, she died,but only after months of excruciating pain.

Dona Marta came each summer at the end of the season to see the beautiful young dancers and let her memories flow over her. She was a riot, though, and not morose at all. Her happy face looked down on us all summer from a portrait in the dining room. There, with morning sun streaming in, we would have our coffee, croissants, fruit, cereal, trying to eat sensibly and not gain an ounce. Before the blistering heat wrapped all around the villa, we took class, worked the barre, stretched every muscle to its safest limit as our bodies remembered the strains from yesterday, the blisters screamed or abated, the soles of our feet arched, working up our legs, thighs stomach, chest, back, head.

We looked ahead as if a kiss awaited, we bent to find the most precious flower, we turned into the great adventure or love around the corner. We danced.

Music could be jazz, rock, classical, atonal---we needed all the sounds to work their way into us. Our favored place was being in modern, not knowing where.

Keiko and I were not always together and that made our meetings better, both in rehearsal and alone. We had to find our own paths before we could surrender to someone else. She was more sinuous and delicate. Her hands were never wrong and her arm bowed in a beautiful arch. Her small bones held her close to the ground and helped her reach for the sky. When she danced a solo, the room turned to her. She was that lovely.

I came to love the strong thrusts of more modern, abstract dance. I wanted the gorgeous sweeps in groundwork and worked on clear transitions to rise and leap across the stage. Someone said I was a Graham natural; I was not so sure. I was not ready to walk down one road abandoning the others.

The summer concert night came and with our best tights, leotards, and accoutrement, we took the stage before Dona Marta. Our directors were on either side. Small comments and quiet murmurs followed our dance. The local audience was appreciative and cheered for each number. They knew us from their streets and shops and recognized their new friends in a special way. They waved and called to us—not a New York audience! And the flowers came from their gardens.

Keiko and I danced the pas de deux from **Appalachian Spring** that night. It was the perfect blend of her delicacy and my power. Night breezes blew softly over us and the music carried us. It was the best we had ever done and we knew it. Flushed with this sweet satisfaction, we linked arms and bowed together, separately, together. And the night ended.

Later at the champagne reception, Dona Marta beckoned to us to come sit beside her. She looked at us for a while and then said the words that changed our lives.

"You girls love each other very much, sí? And this great love moves from one to the other as you dance. I see no competition here, only great effort to share time, space, no? Bueno. You must stay together in all ways and," here she paused, loving the drama, "you must come back to me next summer. That, I think, will be the last summer for your quiet learning. Then great things await. I know this in my heart."

Well, we wept. Her great confidence and gift of more time and space in which to work and learn meant everything to us. Doubled over in thanks, we babbled at her and she laughed. "Go! Love each other and always dance!"

That was our prayer. To love each other and always dance.

25   Firenze

The company disbanded the next day and the dancers went back to London, to Paris, *to* Madrid, New York. We took the train to Florence and treated ourselves to the city we would love more than any other. Firenze!

In a small pensione just off the Via Pisano we woke each morning to the smell of hot coffee, fresh croissants, and the air of Florence. Before the heat became oppressive we would walk the streets , wandering into Michelangelo in the Accademia, taking in the incredible birthday cake that is the Duomo, studying the tiny Biblical figures on the Baptistry and generally behaving like tourists. We were anonymous; we were not dancers. Holding hands we explored the open markets near the Uffizi, went back again and again to the paintings within.

Sunset, though, was not a time for churches or art. It was a time for lovers along the Arno, taking a passamiento. Nodding to passersby, looking into the river's depths.

The passage across the River Arno offered the best jewelry we had ever seen. Bracelets, rings, earrings, pendants, perfect baubles beautifully made. In one tiny shop we lingered over the exquisite rings. We each chose one and looked into each other's eyes knowing what they meant.

Out on the bridge, just as the sun disappeared, Keiko slipped the ring she selected onto my finger whispering, "This is as round and eternal as my love for you. We are one. No wind can ever blow us apart. I love you."

Tears filled my eyes as I held Keiko's trembling hand and gave her my ring. I think I said, "You complete me. Thank you for giving me my life. I will always love you."

We ate well that night and fell into each other's arms for our honeymoon.

What was to be our last year at Juilliard is now a blur of classes, performances, new members, challenging dances that Keiko and I plunged into. Both of us knew the rigors would harden our dancing core, give us the physical memory we needed to deepen as we chose our future repertoire, convinced it would be modern.

Our last summer at the Villa in 2001 was a little like coming back to camp. Some familiar places, some new, re-visiting the creaky villa stairs, capacious kitchen, selecting the same bedroom with its valley view of the vineyards. Our repertoire had changed and we were ready for new combinations. That summer we danced not so much with each other as with the whole ensemble and maybe it was that shift that made us better people. Dance is not about solos or special pas de deux, but about learning every body, every strength and flaw in one's company.

Like a flock of geese, some lead and then tire and swiftly someone else must move to lead the flock. Keiko sensed this before I did and I often saw her after class working with a younger dancer, arching her back as model, lifting a leg, an arm, making small adjustments.

At dinner one night over forbidden pasta and good local wine, she confided that she really wanted to teach. "I want to dance until I can't, of course, but I see more dancers teaching at the same time or in vacation periods. It makes me see what I do through different eyes and break every move into tiny parts. I like that. I am surprised, because I didn't think I would."

The future. The great unknown for everyone, but a special worry for a dancer. We can dance only so long in perfect health. Then, as moves become more painful, the parts change, we dance less, we may be principals, but in a diminished way, receding for the new and young. A serious injury can end it all in a second. Our bodies are our instruments. I had been looking ahead, too, and Dad had chimed in.

"Doll, you need to plan now for what you'll do later. I like the business degree you can get so you can be an administrator later. What do you think?"

"You've been on the computer again, haven't you?" I smiled.

"Yup. You're all I've got. What else would I Google?"

I promised I'd check it out and it really was the best plan. Juilliard may have snarky girls at times, but even they knew the future was shaky for dancers, especially with the number of companies shrinking and openings even more limited.

Anyway, the final week of that summer was special. Dona Marta was in full force, treating us to special light lunches, providing beautiful costumes for the summer gala and generally beaming, as a fairy godmother should. She had Keiko and me to tea one hot afternoon on the piazza. Cool drinks, tiny cakes, and fruit all exquisitely served on thin china.

"I have been observing both of you, you know. Closely. I see you have grown up since last year, no? Si. You still love each other and that is good. It helps the soul, the body, the dance. These things I see. Tomorrow at the gala more visitors will be here. One is the artistic director of the Martha Graham Company. In my mind, I see you with her in New York. You are still young, but we will see. She has been known to invite and give scholarships. Dance your best, bambinos. Now, eat some cakes. They are so tiny!"

That August night was right out of Shakespeare's **Midsummer Night's Dream**. Titania and Oberon held court and we fairies danced across the lawns. Fireflies lit up the night. Mothers held restless children; our local neighbors made quiet noises of appreciation and then lustily applauded each dance. Keiko did things I had never seen before.

And I, well, I was on fire. It was as easy as breathing. Every move flowed into the next and I never thought or worried. I knew I could do no better, at least not now.

With a hand gesture, Donna Marta beckoned us at the performance close.

"I want to introduce you to Janet Meehan, the Artistic Director of the Martha Graham Company. Janet, these are the dancers I have described to you and tonight you saw for yourself. Keiko Ishikawa and Cara Kinslow."

We offered our prettiest bow and heard the magic words, "I was very impressed tonight. Would both of you consider joining our company? Our New York season begins in the spring so you could study with us at Graham School until the opening and be ready."

26 Write Everything Down

Keiko had finished her Juilliard years and now I had, too. She left before I did to attend to housing changes for us and clear all of our stuff out of Juilliard. We made a reunion date for lunch in two weeks, kissed goodbye and she flew off to New York.

She forgot a few things in the wardrobe and I found myself wearing her deep blue scarf every day, smelling her in it, holding her close to me. I still have that scarf and can't dance without seeing it every day. A funny talisman, but looking back, it was as though she left it behind on purpose.

Once a dance program ends, everyone scatters quickly. It was as though we had never been there and the village was quieter. I had a few days of cushion before leaving and I mulled over my future,

walking through vineyards, exploring small shops.
I bought Keiko a necklace with seed pearls I
thought she'd like.

If I started work in the accelerated program at
Graham, I could be in the more advanced Graham II
by the end of the year, be paid and actually perform.
Keiko would be with me on the same track. I
worried about coming to Graham on uneven
footing with the other school members, but I
guessed everyone had stories, some with
scholarships, some without. I would have a lot to
learn and needed to keep a low profile.

Dancers can be jealous and hateful when
aggravated. A clot of jealousy arose in Juilliard
right after we were invited to Italy. Be careful of
rising too fast in this world. Silence falls when you
enter the rehearsal room. Your spot at the barre is
filled. Backs turn and casual lunches do not include
you. Dirty towels can arrive at your locker. Silence
when you enter the rehearsal room. Childish?
Perhaps, but bitter and intentional. It's all very
indirect but the aim is true. The cumulative effect
had been toxic and while we both learned
enormous amounts from the wonderful faculty, the
return to Italy had reinforced our confidence.

Onstage, it is harder to subvert because it is so
public. But there are late entrances, awkward turns.
In the dark, there be dragons. Dragons with long

hair pulled into tight buns with every hair controlled.

Separated, Keiko and I relied on our cell phones. It was too costly from NY to Italy, but when I got into Newark airport, there were her text messages.

- Got us out of Juilliard. Stuff in apt 4 now. Hurry home!
- Lead on Brooklyn apt got 2 decide 2day. Think it is great. Trust me on this 1!
- OK WWrld noon tomorrow. All love,all ways. M

Tomorrow was now today thanks to my screwed up flight delays so I decided to go straight to our lunch reunion, too excited to do anything as mundane as checking apartments. I took a chance and sent my luggage by cab to the old apartment and checked that our doorman really got it. Amazingly, the cab made it and all was good.

The sky was a perfect blue and whatever temperature it was, I wanted it just to stay that way. New York---crisp, always new, fresh, alive, fast. It took two hours to navigate by bus from Newark to the Port Authority, get a Metrocard, catch the train downtown, and let the jet lag smack me. I was exhausted and needed coffee. From the Starbucks on Canal, I called Keiko and got her.

"Hey, you," she smiled over the phone. "Welcome home! Where are you?"

"I'm on Canal getting a muffin and coffee. What time is it, anyway? My clocks are screwed up. I think it's 7:45 but that's a maybe. I decided to come downtown and hang out until lunch. I want to get through the day so I can sleep tonight and get back to normal. Maybe if we show up early it will be even better to get in?"

When the second tower fell, deflated like dusty playing cards with people crashing past birds to the cement below, the water beneath the Brooklyn Bridge glistened with white foam unusual for September. Everyone felt the warm sun, and the sky—why, the sky was an azure blue that made the East River and the Hudson alive with the most precious medieval color of all, the blue of heaven and Mary's cloak. Keiko died that morning, walking into Windows of the World restaurant to make a reservation for our lunch a little later that day. The tables would have been set with the beautiful china of moons and stars. Pieces showed up in the rubble.

"OK, actually I am going into the North Tower now for a meeting with that grant guy I told you about and then I'll just go up. They have breakfast going and I have a surprise for you that I think will be ready. It involves pastry, so get set. So, it's 8 now...9:30? I promise to call if I get done sooner. Keep your cell on."

"Great. I 'll walk by the river a bit and then be up. Can't wait to see you. I love you."

"Back at you."

And she was gone. She did not say the words "I love you." I am left with memories and faint echoes. Nowhere in this universe can I hit repeat and hear her say I love you. Nowhere but my heart.

September 11 is history now but for me it is still an ache in every organ of my body, every day. Time heals? Bullshit.

My Graham brothers and sisters walked the streets for me, doing what I could not. Tadej and Whitney went to the hospitals, asking. Katherine and Heidi put out flyers and Liz attached some to the fence by Trinity Church. Barbara came to cook for me and slept on the couch.

I did not go back to Ground Zero for seven years. I did not care about the other families, the tributes, the architecture.

Bullshit. And fuck it all.

I was not and am not noble. It cannot be comprehended, but why not? I mean, look at Libya, Afghanistan, Egypt, Iraq. I am no more valuable than anyone else.

Keiko Ishikawa was a jewel in God's creation but so were thousands of others.

We just had more media.

So. This is how I remember the day. There are glaring, huge gaps. I can't fix that.

I was so doped for sleep after the flight I think I was drugged. Maybe the goddess of time and space gave that to me because I have fog drifts. When I sleep, some images come back and even though I have a pad by my bed, I still have not captured all the foggy slips. They go too fast and when I have a dream of the day I fear that I have lost a thread forever because maybe it came in the night and I missed the chance to wake up and write it down.

Write everything down. Always.

7:45 I talk to Keiko

8:00 I walk to the Hudson River Park and just sit watching the water lap the pier, watch the Staten Island ferry roll along, close my eyes for a while.

8:30 I start back towards World Trade Center and wonder how to fill an hour. Pick up the **Times** and sit down outside a Starbucks. I don't know what street.

8:46 I look up and see a plane low, too low, in the wrong place and it slams into the North Tower. But that 's where I am going in a few minutes, so that is very wrong. I call Keiko and her phone must be off for her meeting. Does she know? Where is she right this very second? I am here and I can get her out. Now.

No time. Smoke, floating papers, office things, and after a while, people fall down from the tower that holds Keiko. I have to find her and get her to tell me where to go. Everyone is running towards me and soon firemen, cops, turn me away. No lady, don't go in there. I'm dragged back, back. No one to talk to, nothing to say, but if I wait, then I can go back and get her. Get her out.

I am not tired. I can walk forever and it seems that I do. I wound up crossing the Brooklyn Bridge and collapsed outside a deli, dropped like a stone, they say. I hear mumbles and someone gets cold water and the nightmare has just begun. Why doesn't Keiko answer her fucking phone? I kept mine on. She said to keep it on. I kept it on. And the battery is running down so I have to fix that and keep it on. So I can find her. I caress her blue scarf.

The next day I got back to our old apartment and opened the door. Our lives were in boxes everywhere and the boxes stayed taped shut for a long time. I lived with 2 dishes, a mug and plastic spoons for a month. I wore 2 outfits over and over and then I threw them out. I slept all the time.

And then Dad came. Daddy.

27 Cave of the Heart

We did not go to the new apartment in Brooklyn. Dad and I found a small one on 38th on the East side so the trip to Graham was just two subway stops. He stayed two months and then kept coming back. And the liturgy of dance saved my life. I was no fun, I did not want any friends, I danced like a machine, but my arms and legs just took over my soul and I kept putting one foot down after another, hour after hour.

One day in an advanced class a little over a year later, I woke up. Right in the middle of floor exercises. I remember everything Jennifer said that day. It was about 2:00 pm and we were in the middle of floor, not yet moving across the room. We were doing **Night Journey**, the one about Jocasta and Oedipus. Each faces horrible truths as they realize they have been living lies.

I stretched, bending forward, bent to the floor, my head between my legs, letting the muscles grow. The left leg bent, right leg extended, bowing to the floor. My core strength was there.

Still sitting, I contracted, moving forward against the contraction. Martha whispered in my ear, "It all begins with the breath." Breathe, Contract, Release.

I rise with my spine—pelvis, waist, chest, head. And I am a snake with the power working from my lower spine. My hands do not collapse. They are imposing and strong. Hips forward, Martha's ghost gets me ready for long pulls back, leaning out, contracting to center.

A cobra, I do not brace myself. I am ready, in control. I find myself in my cave now, relishing the purest power.

I hear Jennifer berating us with "Come on ladies! Where are you? We are not going anywhere for an hour. Start over!"

She has her hand on Christina's spine, pulling and pushing her head, teaching body to body, but I am somewhere else.

For the first time in one and a half years, I am not trying. I am doing.

7, 8, and 1.

I am in the chorus for **Journey,** a Night Fury, and I am not thinking. It is all visceral from side hinges to turns, to pelvic thrusts. I glaze over looking out at the invisible audience. They may or may not be there and I am looking more down, angled, than at them.

Oedipus will get no mercy or forgiveness from us. The architecture of our group drives him away and we are an organic pulse. The fury of women in a whirlwind. Sideways. Catch. Relevé, relevé, and the deepest grand plié we can get.

"Stop, stop!" Jennifer is talking about the landscape of the human heart, Graham territory.

"It's everything since you've been born, lived, cried, everything you've been through. Fear and anger make a jagged graph of this heart. I can take this down to every move, balance you on each side of your spine, but it has to be yours Release? Why? There has to be a reason, reactive. Abandon counting and open your heart."

I'd heard this lecture before in many combinations, but that day, it shook me back to the joy of dance. I released everything I had felt and let it take me to a new place. I had to explore this new space, but it felt clean and right.

It was time to listen to Martha and "fall, only to rise."

28 Opening Night

After that reincarnation, I was as whole as I would ever be. I joined Graham II, moved right into full Company and had three fantastic years. The Company was back on its feet, literally, after legal battles over Graham's body of work. Energy and joy rippled through the dancers. Even with tension building over the artistic directors, we danced, worried if money would ever come, and looked to each other for the love and support which was there almost palpably.

When I blew my knee out in March 2006, I hated watching from the sidelines. I took class eventually and kept up therapy but hated being out. The fear crept in that this might be the end because you never really know. I was able to take a studio for myself after hours and see how far I could really go. Jennifer and Miki came in and watched me, coached me back and in August, Janet and Virginie finally decided I was good to go. I was afraid at first, but the dances talked me into being brave.

I started teaching then to keep me intact with the work. Watching the young dancers tape toes, cosset blisters, slather on Bengay, dance through beginners' aches made me remember Keiko and me doing the same things at Juilliard. I stopped one late afternoon to talk to Christina from Mexico City, studying in a summer intensive.

She was quiet, her tears just below the surface. She breathed and couldn't talk and she looked up at me. "I just want to dance," she whispered. "Here." Christina had the desire, but from what I could see, the talent was limited and I doubted she would be one of the chosen that season.

"You will dance. Everything that is happening to you here and at home will stay with you and you will draw on it all. I see you improving every day."

Christina smiled then and with a touch on my arm, left to dress.

I mean, how can I crush any hope? Not after what I went through. And, I could be wrong. Christina might fly even yet.

The knee was dicey for two years. But I danced through the pain, eventually taking parts in **Acts of**

Light, Appalachian Spring and **Primitive Mysteries**. It was that last ballet that touched me most deeply. We use what we have: our bodies, sound, rhythm, silence, space, stillness. Several times in this ballet, Martha sanctifies space by placing one toe on the floor and letting the foot fall in place. Here.

Hail Mary, full of grace. Mary. She was born to suffer, to stand at the cross and watch her baby die. In this ballet, she is surrounded by women as acolytes, blessing her, accompanying her into the ultimate pain: the death of her son. The women become bells, swinging gently around her. When Mary falls, these women catch her, hold her. At the foot of the cross, her legs lock; movement is excruciating.   Finally, in her luminous white linen gown, she adopts a Buddha pose with one hand extended upward to receive daily graces and lets the other hand open. She is ready to accept divine wisdom and send it on a flowing current to those who wait. Us. Amen.

She and many other women in the Catholic Church matched my hope for the full humanity and wisdom that only comes from women. I had been to Catholic schools, like my cousins, but when the Church declared me inhuman as a lesbian I couldn't get out the door fast enough. And of course, the Church could never be wrong. In the catechism it is clear, in black and white: "The Church cannot err in what she teaches as to faith or morals, for she is our infallible guide in both." Fine. My spirit is in air and dance. I worship in flight. In **Primitive Mysteries**, I walk with Mary and learn to fall into waiting, loving arms.

Sadly, when I learned about all the priests involved in sexual abuse, I knew I could never return.

These dances and time itself moved my mind and soul to new planes. Not only was I dancing, I was ready to create some original work. When I saw the New York State Arts Commission fly an ad for new works that would have particular impact for New York City, one that could "Easily be performed in multiple sites with low expense," wheels starting turning and I decided to apply for the $20,000 grant.

And so, when I got the e-mail from Norah in November 2008 asking about Christmas, I thought, "Why not?" I was at a juncture of sorts with the grant application brewing. I was ready to create a dance and my uninvited healing time had evolved into several layers of healing, it seemed.

Here's the application as I finally filled it out:

IN 500 WORDS OR LESS EXPLAIN YOUR PROPOSED DANCE. THIS IS A LETTER OF INQUIRY.

IF CHOSEN YOU WILL BE ASKED TO FILL OUT A FULL APPLICATION.OFFER A SUMMARY HERE. 500 word limit

I envision an empty stage. As a prelude, we hear an oboe and piano playing **Ode Number 3** by Kishi . Silently, 10 dancers enter from both sides of the stage, in lines. They do not talk or acknowledge each other in any way. They walk in varying rhythms. They stop. The music stops. One by one they drift off stage, leaving a single dancer. She sways back and forth, bends deeply, rises. This is repeated five times. Music (**Tension** by Kishi) begins, quite lively. Excerpts from Britten's **Simple Symphony** also are heard intermittently. She moves to it slowly and out of rhythm at first and then abandons her self to the driving beat. There is silence. She is still. She dances now, in moves to be created. She engages in wrenching sweeps and arches her back as far back as it can extend. She returns to an upright position slowly, in silence. Ultimately, all 10 dancers return. Now they nod and sometimes bow to each other. Movements become more circular than angular and circles intertwine and dissolve.

I mean to reference 9/11 indirectly with a theme of rebirth after loss. This is a day all adults will remember but in this work I want it to be accessible to children, for even they know being alone, losing something good and then learning to like new people. I want to incorporate a water feature as well. Puppets and veils will waft through the dancers, some to return, some not.

It was mailed and gone, so I could visit an odd strand of my life on Shelter Island.

There, Marian asked me to go to Costa Rica and that, too, fell into the why not category. Strange doors were creaking open for me and it felt good to walk through them. Like Alice, I could only wonder at the other side and see if I was too small or too large. And I was finding a family of my women.

How did I begin my dance? I was just paying attention to...everything. Everything I heard, saw, touched, smelled. Acute heightened awareness made me alert. Made me alive, I guess. The radio played "**With You or Without You**" while I did the dinner dishes one night and I swayed to it, turned up the volume and just started dancing around my kitchen, into the living room, back to the kitchen to notch up the sound and then just let the moves overtake me. I didn't cry. I knew Keiko was in this mix.

Tickets abound at Graham for other events and I found myself watching Ailey, Jones, 360, Paul Taylor, and letting all the variations soak in. One problem in a masterwork driven program like

Graham is that we devote ourselves to the masterpieces of Martha Graham, trying to inhale her air, body, while thinking and still stamping the dances as our own, somehow. This is not easy. But she knew that every body moves differently and one's height, weight, agility all factor in to the final performance.

I looked carefully at my body one night and I saw this in the mirror:

> 5"6""
> 130 pounds
> long brown hair
> muscular arms
> developed thighs
> long legs
> long feet
> small breasts

This was my instrument and any dance I created would come from it. And, you know, it looked and felt fine.

New York Times. September 20, 2009.

By Patricia Kinney
Graham Grant Winner Echoes 9/11

In response to the New York Arts Commission grant opportunity, four New York dancers offered their winning compositions in a blended program with the Martha Graham Company at the Joyce Theater last evening.

Each piece was intriguing, but the most engaging and profound dance was Ms. Cara Kinslow's work entitled "One Soul," that pays homage to her Graham roots and simultaneously moves us to new territory.

Her stated intent to revisit the tragedy of September 11, 2001 in terms accessible for the very young and very old materializes in simple moves counterbalanced by intricate patterns and evocative music. Blending in the infrequently heard classics of Mai Kishi, Ms. Kinslow suggests the patterns of loss, grief and rising from pain in accessible and moving form. Her deft incorporation of water elements in a backdrop cascade and Buraku puppets moving among the dancers holding silk scarves wafting up, moves to include all elements and the invisible. Ms. Kinslow happily avoids the maudlin and offers simple hope.

29 Cinc

Cara danced through Europe that autumn and the company enjoyed unaccustomed acclaim. Europe loved them! Greece became a real possibility for the future and a schedule of college visits balancing the coasts each year fell into a stable pattern. Graham leadership developed teaching kits accessible through the Kennedy Center in Washington, D.C. so the Graham legacy could continue. And new choreographers were aligning with Graham to produce original works. Winds of change were moving the company along and Cara with it.

It was in Paris that another door opened for Cara, almost in her face.

Just outside St Germain des Pres, in the small plaza of nearly bare trees, November leaves blew up and around her as she fixed her path to go back to a small shop of porcelain figures two blocks over. The door of a religious goods store blew open in the wind and a small, black poodle scampered out, making a beeline for the larger boulevard around the corner.

A petite Frenchwoman, arms full of packages, ran to the door and called to Cara, "Madame! S'il vous plâit? That it is my dog! You will get it?" Her eyes matched the pleading tone of her voice.

Cara ran. Nice long legs came in handy off stage once in a while and this puppy would be caught. She scooped up the growling dog who tried to nip her and get away again.

"No, no monsieur. You go to your Mama." Cara spoke in soothing tones to the poodle who decided to lick her vigorously.

Laughing, Cara presented the now happy pup to its owner.

"But I am so embarrassed. Merci, merci! How I can thank you? So many packages for Christmas, you know? It was my job to get this petit miscreant, this naughty dog, not yours." The woman took the dog into her arms and chastised it in what sounded like pretty loving words.

"Not a problem. What is his name?"

"This tres mal chien is called George Cinc. I love this hotel and we cannot afford it. So, Cinc will have to do."

Cara laughed and the wind blew harder.

"Well, good luck and Joyeux Noël."

"No, this is not enough. Just up a small way is a wonderful brasserie. It is very nice and warm inside. A chocolat in thanks?"

And so Cara, Cinc and Jeanne Marie Benoit walked to the brasserie, settled the dog at their feet and talked over chocolat, each stealthily slipping tiny biscotti treats to Monsuier Cinc, then deux vin rouge and they soon slipped into dinner.

Jeanne Marie came to every performance and soon Cara knew she had found a new love. After years of doubting she could love again, Cara immersed herself in a tiny French woman, thanks to an errant poodle. It made no sense, but there it was. They came to revere the church of St. Germain later and decided they were each other's Christmas gift.

They decided to splurge on a night at the Georg Cinc and meet each other in the lobby. Jeanne Marie had been at her design house all day and Cara finished an afternoon rehearsal and rushed over to the beautiful hotel. Sitting in the lobby, waiting for Jeanne Marie, Cara reflected on the past year with gratitude. So many new hearts in her life.

She spied Jeanne Marie coming in through the grand doors and ran to her, sweeping her into her arms. "You are frozen and beautiful! Look how perfect you are!" They hugged warmly and approached the desk.

"Madame?" The clerk looked removed and unimpressed.

Jeanne settled on their reservation in French and turned to keep talking to Cara. They drifted off a few steps only to hear the disapproving clerk call out "Voulez-vous une clé?"

They did indeed want that key and made very good use of the luxurious bed.

Elle est complete.

The Three Graces: Ireland

We were not riff-raff or children of a lesser God.
Magdalene Laundry inmate

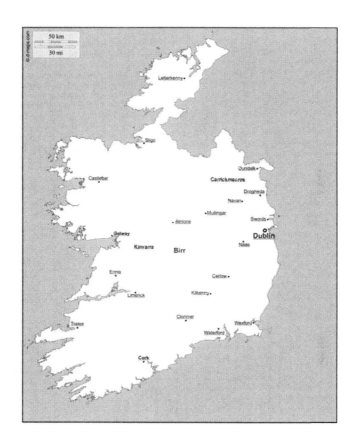

30 Magdalene Laundry

April 2009. Cara in Ireland

Norah's Diary

March. I need to catch my breath. It's amazing how fast things can happen when you set them in motion.

The house sold in one week.

I thought the market had tanked, but on a fluke, this old house went. The friends of Tim,my Peconic Avenue neighbor, fell in love with the old wreck. And for over a million! The value was truly in the waterfront land. Dad would never believe it. I thought I'd have time, maybe even change my mind, but the avalanche started.

Pack. Throw out. Goodbyes---not all that many here on the island, more in the city. I told Sebastian at Bonham's that I just didn't know when or if I'd be back. What a good man he is. He hugged me hard, looked into my eyes and told me to find out whatever I needed to know. I could come back any time.

"The old books here will just be more valuable, and so will you."

So here I am in Dublin in the Grantham Hotel on Grafton St. trying to outline what it is I do need to know.

The more I sorted out the house, my fury rose. Marian and Cara know only the tip of my personal iceberg. As far as I can set up a chronology, this is what I found.

1953: Margaret Mary Lynch marries Joseph Brach. Move to East Rockaway.

Joe develops construction work

Margaret continues to work at Doubleday Publishing in Garden City

1965: They apply for adoption in NYC; told they may not have prompt consideration

1967: articles appear in NY papers on Irish adoptions

1968: apply to Monsignor Jeffers, a family friend, for help. He agrees after seeing their home and financial report and interview on Catholic intentions for the child

1968: November. Letters sent to St Patrick's in Dublin

1970: February. I arrive at JFK airport in NYC
The birth certificate was in English and Gaelic:
Deimhniu breithe ar na h-eisiuint de bhun na
    hActa um Chlaru Breitheanna 1863-1972
Birth Certificate issued in pursuance of Births
    and Deaths Registration Acts 1863-1972
My name was Ann, born to Ellen Malone.
Mom kept these letters in a small box left in the
attic. In the box were tiny, soft leather shoes I wore
when I arrived, small gloves and a lamb. I
remembered that lamb and have it with me now.

> What else do I remember? I was two, but I do
> have shadows of memories---flying at night,
> being cold, holding on to the hands of the
> woman who delivered me here and then, in the
> dark, being held by someone new.

> The questions I have now are these:

> Where are my birth mother and father?
> Why was I left?
> Why that orphanage?

Who was Father McIntyre and what are
Magdalenes? (Both mentioned in one of the letters
as: "Father McIntyre signed the release for this
child" and "Mother consigned to Magladenes.")

> That is all I have for now. Every question takes
> me down dark roads.

March 11.

Great breakfast here at the Grantham Hotel.

The waitress was about 50 years old and had worked here for years. I began my detective work over my tea.

"I wonder, could you direct me to the St. Patrick Home?

"Well, now, that I can. Would you be wanting the Guild or St Pat's on the Navan Road?"

"Navan Road, I think."

"Will you be after adopting a small one then? Not as easy for that these days, you know."

"I think I came from there." That was the first time I had said those worlds out loud to anyone. I gulped some tea and brushed away sudden tears. Get a grip, I told myself.

The waitress filled my pot with more hot water, lay down a fresh scone and took a breath.

"Aye. Well, in older days, many babies left from there on to grander days in the USA. I'm thinking you were one of those. My aunt was a nun there and she was one of the good ones. Not all of them nuns were as good as they seemed."

"How so?"

"I shouldn't be saying that now, should I? I am sure they will help you." The directions followed and I left, thoughtful.

Later that morning, I was standing outside St Patrick's Home. It was a grey stone house of three stories in a solid block. Windows were curtained. It was something out of **Jane Eyre** without a pretty plant anywhere. March wind blew down my coat and I shivered.

The registrar at the home desk was all business when I arrived. She looked at my letter and notes and left the room without a word. She came back with a handwritten ledger with 1970-72 on its black spine and opened to a page that she carefully covered with plain white paper above and below the lined entry she pointed to.

"To preserve privacy, you see. You've no need to see any other names at all. There you are. You can copy it off if you like."

She stood, starched wimple clenching her tight little face and her busy blue eyes clamped onto me, watching my face for some response, I suppose.

I saw: girl. 1 yr. Anne Maloney. Transferred from Mother of Good Counsel Home, Limerick, per request Father Delaney of St. Mary's Parish Galway. Mother deceased. Moira Ellen Maloney.

Galway? Limerick? Mother died? It was all confusing and disturbing but I wouldn't let that thing of a nun see me startle.

"Are you sure that is me? The names don't match with what I have."

"Some errors came in over the years, but this is the closest name to what you are asking after that I can see. And Father Delaney was a regular monitor in those days. There's nothing more I can tell you. Now. I must be off and hope that satisfies you?"

So, I had started life elsewhere, wound up here and was sent to the US all in two baby years.

I met her cold glance calmly.

"Well, you've been just great. I'd like to look around a bit, if that's all right."

She paused. "You may walk the grounds."

 I walked out to the chill Dublin wind.

This cold block has four floors, many narrow windows and no sense of what sort of rooms or wards were behind them. The gardens were bare and an unkempt grotto to Mary was in a far corner of the grounds as though no one knew it was there. Behind the statue in overgrown bushes was a square plot of land unmarked but for a wrought iron fence around it.

The eerie silence absorbed my steps on the
    cobblestone path and my breathing.
Where was everyone? Why was no one walking
    the grounds?
And what was the square plot for?

March 12

Today I went to the General Registry Office in the Irish Life Center on Lower Abbey Street armed with conflicting names and places. It is a huge center and finding the Centre for Irish Life was tricky. I entered off Talbot Street. The initial research is daunting with so many similar names, but the exact combination of places should limit the search a bit. I had little luck as entries before 1966 had not dates and referred me to other volumes. The plethora of repeated and double names with variations was mind-numbing. I did find the original birth certificate for me but no data on my mother's name, death, or address.

I went online to research the word Magdalenes and the stories shocked me beyond belief.

If a girl was unmarried and pregnant, she was at fault. She was dirty and should be shed by any family. But where to put her? The Catholic Church had just the spots: Magdalene Laundries. Named after Mary Magdalene, whom they unjustly pegged as an altogether bad woman, these formidable sites did, in fact, do laundry. The nuns did church laundry of altar linens, crisply starched priestly robes, some hotel laundry and prison laundry. The unforgivable girls who came there in shame did all the work. Their life goal was to attempt to repent as did Mary Magdalene.

Standing for up to 12 hours at a stint, they hand-washed every bit of fabric assigned to them. Backs aching, hands stinging, they labored on. At night, they were told to line up naked. The nuns would walk up and down the line, snickering at pubic hair (Oh she has lots to go on with, doesn't she), breasts (Nice big juicy ones there. No wonder you are here, you slut.) The humiliation was deep and cruel.

Girls never left. If a man came for them, a father or brother, perhaps a few got out, but why would any man come? They were the very ones who threw them away.

The babies? Some women signed papers in hopes of sending their babies to America and truly believed they were fat and happy children in the USA. In truth, not many left because they died of neglect and malnutrition. Some were sent to other laundries. They were buried in mass graves on laundry grounds along with the fortunate women who also died as their last relief.

All of this is visible evidence of the Church's twisted obsession with all things sexual. Not a shred of human sympathy or love appeared at these laundries.

And my rage doubled as I realized that I was born in one of them.

31 Eucharia

The same waitress was on duty at dinner that night and asked about my hunt. I told her a few of the details and confusion and she fell quiet.

"I work until 9 tonight. Would you fancy a glass at the corner pub?"
I would at that, and waited for the time to pass.

Later, over a Guinness and a Shandy, Mary Fleury talked.

She told me of the Magdalenes, the shifting about in Ireland of mothers and babies, and alerted me to *Justice for Magdalenes*, a site I had seen online earlier. She wrote down on a slip of paper "Mother Eucharia, Sacred Heart Convent, Limerick" and told me to see her.

"She's a good old girl who entered with my aunt, Sister Gerald, donkey's years ago. She's retired now but has all her crackers and a few chocolates will open her right up. You need to know what she has to say."

We parted with a hug and I got ready to leave Dublin.

Next morning, I called Marian and left messages that it would be fantastic if she could come over now. The hunt was quickening and I did not think I could go it alone much more.

Rain splashed my rented Mini next morning and it took me three hours to get to my next bit of hope, Limerick.

Limerick, 2 days later. Norah's Diary

Lots to report. The rain turned into a true downpour for most of the day and I took refuge in a pub on the High Road. I peered into the darkness of the main bar and heard a quiet voice say "And is it the lovely weather that brings you here, little one?"

Behind the voice was a tall, gangly barman, all smiles. "I am here to see the orphanage and will need a place to stay for a few days. Can you help?"

"That I can. Give me a little minute. Upstairs is the snuggest bed to be had in all of Limerick. Away from the bustle of the high road and shops, so. My Caitlin has it covered in quilts and blankets. We'll put you there and be serving you a grand breakfast when you wake."

It all sounded good and I settled in and checked my e-mails. Thankfully, Marian was on her way straight from Costa Rica!! What a gift. I decided to go on my own the next morning to the next step— the Good Shepherd Laundry. But before I went there, I called the Sacred Heart Convent as directed by my friendly waitress to see if Mother Eucharia was up for a visitor. After a wait, the nun came back to answer that the sister would, but only briefly as she was not too well.

Armed with a small box of dark chocolates purchased from the chemist down the street, I knocked at the convent door. The housekeeper let me into the front parlor and asked me to wait. Soon, a tiny, stooped nun in full habit walked in slowly She appraised me in silence and then asked "Now what can I be doing for you, young lady?"

"Little one" and "young lady" all in a day, I thought. I struggled to find the right words into the mystery.

"I was told that you served in the Good Shepherd Laundry some years ago—around 1970? Sister Mary Gerald's cousin, Mary Fleury, sent me to you."

The nun relaxed somewhat at that name. "Ah well, sure I did. And Gerald was a great one to be with, God rest her soul. She played a great game of tennis."

Marian began her saga. "I am trying to find my mother. A family in New York adopted me in 1970. I have a letter from the St. Patrick's Home in Dublin, but some notes confuse me as they mention Limerick as well. Can you help me?"

She looked past me into the rainy street. Cars passed and street sounds filtered in a muffled way. She spoke very softly.

"Yes, that may have been so. We had a terrible influenza in 1969 and we sent some of our babies to Dublin for a safer place. It was quite a to do. You were probably one of them and it's pleased I am that you had a good life in the states. It was good? "

"Well, I had good parents and now they are dead. I only discovered my adoption after my mother died and I was clearing things out." I looked away.

"Are you angry, then? I think you are."

"Yes, I am. Angry that I lived a lie all these years and angry I was left, angry I do not know who I am."

She patted my hand. "Why, darling, you are yourself. It may well be your parents loved you so fiercely they wanted you all to themselves. Did you ever think that could be it?"

"It feels more to me that they did not trust me to love them. Or that they worried I would leave them."

"It's a thorny road. I can tell you this: we did many things wrong over the years for our innocent babies. Ireland was so sure it was right in every moral crease it could find and judged our women too hard. I was told to shut up about this, but I can't. What can they do to me now? I remember a girl from Birr many years ago because we did not get many girls from there. Her name is gone, but I know she had a baby girl. Now, in those days from the time I was a young nun, we were on a mission to save the sinners as we saw the unwed mothers to be. Our order worked to keep them in our laundries forever, working off their terrible sins so they would be sure to see Heaven.

I had my doubts, but it was my order and I went along, trying to see the good of it, don't you know. Some of the women left when a man would come to claim them—a brother or uncle usually—never a father for wasn't it them who brought them here all in shame in the first place.

For you, my girl, I just do not know for sure. You may be the bairn from Birr I remember. If I caused you pain and sorrow, I ask you now to forgive me. I did what I was told was best."

I could not hate her. She, at least, had thought it out and had raised her voice courageously when no other religious did.

"You did right, Sister. I do not need to forgive you. Just pray for me now as I try to find out if my mother is dead or alive."

"I will that." And she slipped into my hands rosary beads of smooth wood. "Do you know this? Yes? Well, then, your mother is taking care of you still."

She stopped. "Both of your dear mams. God bless you in your journey."

I hugged the tiny nun. "And, truly, God bless you, sister."

32 Dirty Laundry

April 25

Today I rested and walked about the city, waiting for Marian to arrive. I drove into the green countryside around the city and tried to imagine my pregnant mother coming there on the road from Birr. What had she seen and felt beyond despair and fear? I bought soda bread and double cheddar cheese with a sausage for my lunch on the road.

I finally faced what was to come. My mother could be dead. I might never find her or her grave. She could be alive, somewhere not too far away, maybe having a cup of tea right now. That last possibility gnawed at my most.

And my anger has not abated. I feel angry with my adoptive parents, with my birth mother, and with the Catholic Church for supporting the whole sham. I knew then that I was without a church. On my own.

I reviewed my research on Magdalene Laundries and set the horrors in place in my mind. Details now fleshed out the bare outline I had to that time. Founded in the 1800's by several religious orders of nuns, these places were to be a refuge for sinners—the unmarried mothers of Ireland. They were brought there by shamed parents who often disowned these girls, never to see them again. A girl could be sent just for being pretty, because she was probably going down that sinful path eventually and was "an occasion of sin" for some unsuspecting lad. The men involved skipped off, of course.

The laundries really did do wash. Linens, tablecloths, church linens, hotel sheets all came to the back gates and were laundered by the women inside, standing at long, low tubs, hand washing all the filth away. An inmate would rise at 5AM, go to mass, and have a short breakfast of bread and tea. Then the backbreaking work set in without conversation, without breaks until 7pm when they dropped into bed, exhausted.

Most women had their heads shaved as a reminder that external beauty did not match their sinner souls. They were forced to bind their breasts with tight calico strips and wear shapeless dresses, thick stockings, and hob-nailed boots. They were humiliated and ridiculed by the ever-watching nuns who sometimes had them stripped naked for mocking perusal of who had the hairiest body, who had the largest breasts.

Early foundresses wrote the women were not to be beaten, but they were. Belts came off the nuns and cracked the backs.

The last of the laundries closed in 1996. So the buildings remained, some put to newer uses like homes for the mentally challenged.

My references so far had brought me to the St. Patrick's Charity home in Dublin that sent me to New York in 1970. I must have been one of the last to go, since by 1972 Ireland had started supporting single mothers with limited stipends. So, as the secular revolution hit Ireland, women became more emancipated and knowledgeable of their rights, public outcry railed against sending Irish babies away, and later, publicly revealed the shameful laundries for what they were.

The cryptic notations I saw at St. Patrick's had led me here to the Limerick location where my mother started her ordeal. This place was run by the Sisters of Charity and now it seemed possible that a flu epidemic had sent me off to Dublin. But my mother remained and must have wondered where I was. What had she been told? That I was dead? Adopted and sent to somewhere in the States?

Interviews with laundry victims that I watched online through tears exposed how dearly the babies were missed. On woman said she would stand at the back gate and ask if anyone had seen her baby at all. They would stand on the flat roof and search the streets. Some of the babies were in the very buildings where their mothers worked, but they could not see them. They were never allowed conversations among themselves, as that would have led to greater and vocal dissatisfaction and rebellion. Secret, secret. Damn and damn.

33 The Power of Two

By the next day, Marian had taken a bus from Shannon Airport to Limerick and was eager to help. Fortified by a huge Irish breakfast complete with eggs, gammon, potatoes, tomatoes, breads and jam, Marian and I set forth to do battle. I caught her up on all I knew so far and her complete, deep silence as she listened told me her heart was in knots. When I finished, we just held each other and cried for all the injustices dealt here. Then she handed me this letter. The new Shelter Island owners had found it in a closet and got it to Marian as my U.S. contact.

Feb.10, 1970

Dear Kathleen

    We're now in Dublin. The room is damp no matter what I do, no matter how many coins I drop in the heater. I cried the first night when no heat came at all and I had no idea we needed to feed this fake heater. Joe had to roust up the manager, who laughed. We should have gone for a fancier hotel but this trip plus the "donation" we are expected to give is very expensive.

    I mention the room since I am here so much. We wait for final calls from the St. Patrick Home. We don't go out together lest we miss the phone. Joe has been to the library and seen the Book of Kells. So have I, just not together. We have seen the Post Office from the rebellion and can actually see bullet holes in the wall. We are just not tourists at all. All this is to say I am trying to distract myself from the dreadful waiting. I have such a dark sense that it will all crash down and they won't let me have my baby. My dark Irish corridors, I suppose.

    The nuns were direct and bossy about this procedure. They did perk up when they saw our check for $5,000. I know that one false step and that bitch Sister Bridget would slap me. That freezing cold parlour of theirs would freeze a witch's teat. I don't know why the nuns make me so sad, they just do. I think they must be doing good for so many pregnant girls from all over Ireland, but I feel deep down that something is very wrong here. But it's with the Church and they know the best, right? It's a test of faith, I'll tell you.

I just want that baby girl in my arms and I'll run, run home. But if all goes well, Joe and I go home and the baby is delivered in a month or so. We were told that this extra visit would help, so we came.

I think that you really do understand how empty my arms have been. You had your baby girl so quick, so easy. Why couldn't Joe and I manage this ourselves? There's no test to take, just Dr. Dursley taping my knee and patting me on the shoulder telling me to "relax" and "trust God."

Joe says he wants this little girl as much as I do, but I'm not sure. Sometimes I think he's doing this for me because I'm so desperate. I cry at odd times for no reason at all.

I want to call her Norah.

I'll say goodnight.

Love,

Maggie

That was a lovely piece to help me re-focus my parents. I was desperately wanted. They were not the bad guys here, but someone sure was.

We were in no mood for crap from nuns, I'll tell you.

Got to the Good Shepherd Home and were met with stony looks, long waits, incorrect records brought to us, general vagaries meant to send us off. I persisted with the note from the St. Patrick record about this home as the original source and demanded all the record books from 1969-72 or else I would get court orders and involve the press.

The books came, slapped down in front of us. The nun tightened her wimple and marched off.

Marian suggested looking for any possible variation on the name "Mary, Maura, Moira,Ellen Malone" and we dug in.

Three hours later we had narrowed our search to just a few. By eliminating those out of fairly close range, we were left with two:

Margaret Mary Maloney of Birr in County Offalyand Moira Ann Malone of Killucan.

We left the books on the table and drove straight off to Birr as a random first choce, collecting our suitcases on the way.

We got to Birr around 6:00 pm, feeling rode hard and put away wet. Thank God for Irish pubs and the cheerful sounds of life within. After a glass of Jameson, we both relaxed.

I hadn't really asked about Costa Rica but Marian said that story could wait. She had learned some important things about herself, she smiled, and reassured me it was all good news. But, later for that.

Sizzling trout came up for our dinner and we tucked in.

"Are you ready for total failure in all this?" Marian asked quietly.

"I think I am. I want to know that I tried everything and then I will come to terms with whatever I really know. Maybe Mom and Dad suspected this would be a terrible circus trying to untangle the facts and so just let it be. I play our lives together like a tape loop trying to look in from the outside to see if we were ok or not. They were older, of course, and got quite set in their ways, but I think they really did love me, as best they could show it. They were very worried around the time I went to college, and now I see why. They had promised to send me to a Catholic university when they adopted me, and I wanted Columbia in New York. That was one of the few times I saw Mom cry, and I relented. Marywood in Scranton, Pennsylvania was a wonderful experience and the smaller atmosphere suited me. Those were funny, normal, good-hearted nuns and they make me realize these Irish nutters are not the norm.

Spent, we went to bed. Cold Irish air, the clearest night of stars.

34 Truth

From Marian's diary.

I joined Norah today on the final part of her quest, ready to buck her up should we meet with closed doors and no answers.

Birr today is still small with winding streets. On Clonmet Lane behind the high street we stopped in front of the cottage of Margaret Mary Maloney. Norah gave me a hug and went to the door alone. She said she'd call out for me if she needed me there.

I waited. No cows in the lane, but a barn far ahead, open fields and a scraggy little dog peeing on a tree. Very quiet.

I wonder what Norah really will do if she finds this woman. It may not be a tender reunion at all. I think of my own close-mouthed mother and how little I ever really knew about her. That was an interview I wish I could undertake. Maybe that's why I am tagging along here.

Norah came out after a few minutes, waving to the woman in the door who arched her neck curiously to see me.

"No joy there," she sighed. "Nice lady, but no possible link. I guess we're off to Killucan."

The road to Killucan brought us by Lake Ennell where we stopped to drink some coffee and wolfed down ham sandwiches purchased at a small shop in Birr. The lake water spread placidly before us. Hawks soared, letting the air carry them. I remember looking kind of sideways at Norah to see if she was getting more nervous. Out of the blue, she quoted Hamlet: "If it is to be now, it will be...."

I couldn't top that so, we smiled and drove the rest of the way listening to Enya. Soft women's voices seemed the right sound as green hills and open fields slid by.

We stopped at the local church, St Catherine, and knocked at the rectory door. The housekeeper eyed us a bit suspiciously but went to "fetch Father." Father McHugh was young enough and had a friendly smile and open hand to us both.

"What brings you to this part of the bog?" he asked quietly. "Not exactly on the tourist path, are we?"

I let Norah sum up the story as we knew it so far and the priest looked out the side window where four dogs romped about.

"Those were bad times and I am sorry for your pain. I'm not going to pretend all that didn't happen, because I know now it did. It's left to us to try to patch things up, if we can. Let's go on a hunt of the registry."

We sought "Moira Ann Malone," and finally Father McHugh turned back a page and stopped, looking down.

"I think this is what we want. Malone was a family here for some years and we still have a few in the parish. Will I call Johnny for you?"

Yes.

Mum.

35 Mum

Norah could hardly breathe and time slowed to an eerie stillness while the cousins waited for the call's results. A hopeful black lab slobbered over them with her ball, nosing them into throwing it out on the grassy yard. Labs can make anyone laugh and so the women were laughing and throwing balls when the priest came out to them, a tray with tea and cookies set prettily.

He smiled.

"Now, I don't know how this will play out, that's so true, but Johnny is willing to come talk to you. He might be your uncle and he's driving in just now, so."

There are times when all parts of the universe converge and come together as one. This was one of those moments. Tea, cookies, dogs, a helpful priest and a man in a truck on his way. It just felt right. And, it was.

John Joseph Malone was a big man with a red truck and cap in hand. He nodded to the priest with a "Father," and walked right over to Norah.

"I've been looking for you for some time. I want you to know that. You look just like your Mum." With that, Norah let the tears come as she sneezed over and over.

"What's this, then?"

John and Norah laughed and she blubbered that she didn't know, she only did this when she was near cats. John roared in laughter. "That ties the donkey. I have cats and Mum is truly allergic, as well."

It took time but this is what Norah and Marian learned:

Moira Ann Malone had in truth been left at the Limerick Laundry when she was age 18 and pregnant. Her father wanted her to go as far away as possible. Her father never returned for her and he died 8 years later. The other children, John and Patrick were told their sister had died in Dublin and not to talk about it, as it would upset their mother too much. They took it at that, though it seemed queer to have no funeral. When Ellen

Malone,their mother, was desperately ill with shingles, she took Johnny aside and told him in a rambling way to "go find your sister and her baby." It seemed a drug-induced illusion, but the request echoed in Johnny's mind.

Johnny summarized his hunt of many efforts intermittently to crack into the secrecy of the convents, to seek any help he could devise regarding his lost sister.

He coughed to catch his voice and sipped some tea. He looked directly into Norah's blue eyes and in a low voice told her the last bit.

"Finally I traced her to the Good Shepherd Laundry in Limerick and saw her name or close enough to it on the damned register. I demanded to see her that very moment. I didn't give a tinker's damn what they thought. Some old biddy of a nun stomped off and I waited.

Those nuns were right bitches. Every feckin' one of them tried to cover up what was going on. All I knew was that I wanted this one woman out. It wasn't till later I learned what horrors they were about. They tried telling me that sure, she could have gone out at any time but chose to stay and become pure. Pure. Jesus Christ. Pure.

Your Mum was that pale and thin, her hair all scraggily like and she just stood, head down.

She had not one thing with her and I took her by the hand and we marched out of that place, her crying and a wee bit frightened of me. Only natural, that.

She wanted to know where I had been. She called me Johnny. That was a hard road to trot, but I tried to help her see the way of it. She listened hard and patted my hand and said, 'It's all right. I'm out.'

She is a bit queer, some say, but them as know what happened see her as inward, like. She does not talk very much. We gave her a wee cottage behind the house and barn and she likes having her own bits and bobs around her. She walks the four rooms and dusts and protects her china whatnots every day. She likes Irish fairytales. After a while, she asked for school journals and she looked over a few kinds before she lighted on the ones all black and white scrabbled on the outside and all lined paper inside.

'Those are the ones,' she says, and right after goes on with pens and fills five of them, front and back of every page.

We knew she wrote, but she never would talk about the place; that's what she calls it, 'the place.' So. We let her be and find her own space as it was. This was 1990. She's 60 years old. Most days she stays in, checks the chickens, does her jigsaw puzzles a treat and watches telly. "

It had been ten years before Moira let Johnny read her notebooks. She was ashamed of being an ex-Maggie.

Norah asked what actually had happened to Moira in the laundry.

Her uncle opened one of the journals at random and began to read from it.

We always loved it when the bells rang out. It meant someone escaped. The walls were 20 feet high and had glass pieces and metals scraps pointing out from the tops so as nobody could get away. But some did. At night I went to the toilet and that was the only place with a bit of open window so I could see the sky. And I prayed to all the saints, especially Bridget, to help me get out, to fly over the damn walls and find my baby girl. Her name is Ann.

And...

One day I just could not get myself out of bed to work, I was that tired. My hands had all cracked and blistered from the lye soap. Sister Simon came and hauled me out and made me go down. That night I remember Kitty Sheehan crying for me when I had to lie down on the floor in front of everyone with my

arms outstretched like a cross and beg forgiveness.
Kitty never saw her baby, the one she had because
the parish priest raped her."

There was deep silence when John finished. Norah and Marian had no words, just tears running down their cheeks. There was absolutely nothing to say. The dogs lay sleeping then and groaned in their sleep, twitching as they chased squirrels in their dreams. Sunset was glorious that day—all purples and golds deepening to a deep, dusky red. Father McHugh offered supper, but the family left, having had enough of clergy for a lifetime.

The next day, Moira Malone busied herself in her small house. The eggs collected, she sat down for a second cup of morning tea with milk and two sugars. Johnny was coming over soon and she had baked soda bread with the currants he liked. Something to tell me, he said. What could that be, then? Not bad news, she had asked worriedly? No, no, not at all.

And people were coming with him. Now that made Moira anxious. Strangers. They would look her up and down and sometimes she felt like old Sister Gerardus was doing the looking, that nasty smirk across her puss. Was I dirty? Clean. Dressed all right? Hair not too long. She still kept it cut short, the long soft hair on her neck a reminder of how dirty she was. She liked to feel her hair, soft as spring grasses.

Moira had found a way to keep the nuns in her head at bay by turning to a window. She never could get enough of window looking and the true richness of having ten windows of her very own in the house. Ten, when before in the place she had only the broken one in the toilet to look out at night, talking to the stars, talking to her Mam to please come and get her, she'd be good now. Very, very good. If she'd only come.

Outside, luring small kittens to her with a pie tin of cream, Johnny's little Helen Anne lurched about in her wobbly 2 year- old walk. A checked pinafore over her short pants, she giggled as the kittens stuck their tails up and followed her in a circle. Then she plopped down ,the cream spilled, and the kittens were all over her.

I do love that child, Moira thought. Not the damn cats, but that girl has stolen my heart. I had a little girl, too. Ann. So long ago, but I remember the smell of her. I just had her in my arms for a few months and then she was gone. Adopted by nice people in America. Now how large was America? She would see it on the telly and knew it was vast. Was my girl still there? She'd be old now. Just gone forever. No, not today, don't go into that room of my head today. I must be at my best for these people John has.

Someone knocked at the door and Moira opened it to see her brother John and two lovely women with flowers in their hands.

Come in.

The actual words became a blur but Moira saw the truth right away and let the reality flow over her. She sat down. She could not stop staring at Norah.

John began. "Mam, this pretty lady is your daughter, Norah." His voice choked with ready tears.

"Norah? That's a perfect name for you. You are beautiful. Are you really mine?"

John and Marian left Norah and Moira to discover each other alone. They drifted across the yard, scooped up Helen Anne and walked to the barn where the kittens had disappeared.

36 On the Road

A few days later over an extended family meal, the cousins met dozens more cousins of all ages still new to the idea of this family. Laden with salmon, pies and cakes, the dinner table looked full and happy as stories and names and connections appeared.

"I'm full," announced Norah to her brother Johnny, and the smile shared told each other she meant more than apple pie. "I need to make plans about whatever's next."

"And that would be...?" Johnny waited.

"I want to stay on but this village seems in hard times now."

"It is that. Industry has gone off, jobs are few and the lads move out when they can. To South America, a lot of them, in computers of all things. In fact, that is where your brother Pat went."

"Marian is going back to Dublin for an art history meeting and I think I'll tag along. She wants to think ahead now, too. We won't stay together forever, but for now, it sounds like a good idea. But she wants to go tomorrow and I think I'll stay with Moira a bit more, be quiet with her."

"Right for you, then. I have to see my supplier in Dun Laoghaire just south of Dublin and I'll take her along in the truck, if that's o.k."

Marian thought it a great idea, packed up and was ready in the morning, outside the inn, standing in a light rain.

John pulled up and grinned. "Sure and isn't it a grand, soft day? Would you be wantin' a lift on the way?" His exaggerated brogue broke Marian up and she struggled up into the front seat.

They drove along in companionable silence, listening to the radio. The rain picked up a good bit and was no longer 'soft.' It dumped on them and despite herself, Marian was a bit uneasy.

"Is this, um, normal? Pretty dense out there."

John glanced over at her quickly and in that moment the truck lurched out of control and went on a long, fast slide to the right, settling into deep grass and mud.

"Well, no. Shite, this is not normal at all. " With a low "fuck," John clambered out and studied the damage.

"We are for it, I'm afraid. Need to call for help to get her out of this muck. Stay in the cab and I'll see what I can do."

Grabbing his cell phone, John punched in some numbers and soon could report help was on the way. Someone would come from the local auto shop in a car and then get them on their way or back to the repair shop.

"Egg sandwich? " offered Marian, trying to smile. "Why not," sighed John.

The rain kept coming, winds blowing from the west and the grey hedges seemed to shrink into themselves for protection and the mud just got sloppier. With no building in sight, they were stuck good and proper.

"I guess you haven't such weather in California," John proffered.

"On the coast, some days can be brutal, but they are not very often that way. This is really beautiful. It is the wild Ireland I've read about."

John looked at her over his egg sandwich. "You've told me some dabs about what you do, but it's not clear to me yet."

"I study ancient and medieval art and teach art history classes. My dissertation was on Celtic forms and now I'm here, it seems a wonderful chance to renew some friendships at Trinity College and go look more at the Book of Kells. That's where I'm headed now. And I have read about the Island of Iona off Scotland. Legend is that the monks from Iona crafted the Book. I want to go there as well."

"My mother lives on Iona. Kells. A proper beauty, that. I've seen pages a few times on visits. Can you make out the knots and all?"

Marian laughed. "The monks were sometimes tipsy when they did those buggers. One loop usually leads to three more and comes home tucked under another. I like the nasty little men you sometimes see hanging on vines. Rude, and funny."

"Do you paint, yourself?"

Marian paused. "I used to and now, for some reason, I want to again. That's something else to figure out while I'm here. This rain is sure buggering on."

"I think I see lights coming up the road. Maybe our man is come."

Johnny slid from the driver's side and stepped into the rain.

A late model blue Cooper Mini pulled up next to them in their ditch. Poking his head out the window, a black haired man with glasses on asked if they were all right.

"What does it look like, man? Don't be thick." John got out to ruefully survey his sad red truck once again.

The stranger talked a bit and John poked his head in the track cab to Marian.

"This feller says he'll take you on a bit to the village pub just a way down the road. What do you think? He looks ok to me."

Marian was freezing and she pushed aside her reservations about black-haired men in storms and decided to take her chances. She looked the man over again and then got out of the truck.

She checked cellphones with John and with a promise of seeing him shortly, she got into the car of Barry Duffy.

"I'm safe, ma'am. I won't bother you a bit and will just get you to the pub and you can wait for your husband there."

"Oh no—he's my cousin. Yes, he's my cousin," she repeated, saying that for the first time. "Look, I am sure you are being kind but do you have some identification I could see?"

"Just a tick. Of course. Should have offered that straight off. Sorry." He shifted uncomfortably, caught as a potential molester or serial killer and took several cards from his wallet.

"Well, here you see my driver's license so you know it is me. And here is an American Express card so you know I shop. And this, this one is good for letting me work, and here it is." He stopped and proudly offered up his faculty card from Trinity College to Marian, who lit up.

"Fantastic. Trinity is on my list of places to visit and you don't look like the kind of university killer I see on Morse. You know, BBC mysteries? "

"Thank you for that. " He assembled himself, cleared of all murder charges, and started up the engine briskly.

After a while the two talked easily and Marian learned that Barry taught literature classes at the college, though not all the time, and was now returning from a long period of writing at his cottage on the western coast near Galway.

"This guy is intriguing, thought Marian. I'm not sure where all this is going, but I do like him so far." She took a few glances at him and saw a middle-aged man with a shock of jet-black hair and deep blue eyes. Gorgeous.

Once in Dublin proper, Barry dropped Marian back at the hotel where Norah had stayed earlier. They parted with a promise to see each other soon.

When Marian's cell rang the next morning and she heard Barry's nervous voice, she had to laugh.

"Is this my axe murderer scholar? You weren't kidding when you said 'soon'."

Silence hung in the air.

Barry coughed and mumbled something about, "Not sure, so sorry, I'll call later" and more miserable words until Marian laughed and said, "Come on over for breakfast."

Silence. Finally a strangled, "Really? Now? I'm on my way."

Barry and Marian tucked into a full Irish breakfast, she with scone and he with brown bread.

She shared her academic background with him and he brought her up to date on his work.

After tea, Barry looked at Marina closely.

"Sure, I never thought to find a medieval scholar wet as a rat in the road." He laughed. "But I am certainly glad I did."

They parted cheerfully, each hoping for more visits.

Over the next few weeks, Marian found her rhythm. She settled into a flat near the university, small but quaint with a friendly manager. Days found her visiting the Trinity Library a number of times, drawn back to the Book of Kells and its intricate designs.

And she saw Barry rather often.

Dinner in his favorite restaurant in Dun Laoighre by the sea, gobbling down the creamed lobster in their Dublin Lawyers, wandering into James Joyce spots where the author lived and wrote, walks along the Dublin quays all with talk, good, good talk. Each of them seemed to be holding their breath, not sure this new link would hold up.

One night after a revival performance of Shaw's **Mrs. Warren's Profession** at the Phoenix Theater, they emerged to a death grip fog that clamped onto bones. There was no street and all buildings were gone.

"Christ, this is bad," Barry declared and shouted out to dim yellow lights from a cab winding down the street. Having caught the cab, they crept slowly to the nearby Doolan Hotel and restaurant. Two brandies down, Marian put down her glass, traced its damp ring on the wooden bar, looked into Barry's corny blue eyes and winked.

"Let's get us a room and do the deed," she smiled.

One hour later, the deed was well done and they rolled over each other laughing and touching and laughing.

"Jesus H Christ that was brilliant!" pronounced Professor Duffy in solemn tones.

'Do you think you could do that again?" He sounded very hopeful.

Professor Driscoll could and did.

Exhausted, they soon slept like the spoons they were.

No fog remained the next morning and dressed as they were the evening before, they left the hotel, unwilling to part.

"Come live with me and be my love?" intoned Barry.

"I will all pleasures prove, swear to God."

Marian grinned, "I'm sure you would. Let's sort things out and think about next moves. Yes?"

Barry stared her down. "Will you know by tonight?"

A giggle escaped from Marian and in a girlish tone she countered, "No, I shan't. But I'm a quick sorter-outer. You'll see."

37 Cushna House

When Barry had a teaching break, they went to his cottage in Kinvarra. The closer they got to the village, the more anxious Barry became.

"It isn't grand at all. I have been there alone for years and it may be a shabby lot for you. " He tried to remember how clean it was when he left last time. It was all right, he thought.

Marian just listened and said, "No worries." Irish folk music filled the car and the lyrical Irish voices matched the mood Marian was in that afternoon. Sort of mellow and drifting, not anxious, full of contentment. She was curious but not expecting too much from this cottage Barry had inherited from his maiden Aunt Helen. She had not been much of a housekeeper, he had said, and he hoped it was better than when she had tucked things in crazy corners and mended curtains with safety pins. Somewhat better, anyway.

Just before the road dipped into Galway, they were surrounded by hills and a deep gorge before them all covered in mist and fog. The sounds were dense and enclosed, putting them into a thick cocoon. There was no other land or sea. This was all there was. Crags loomed above them with mossy green lichens drifting in a million patches. Rocks encrusted the road's edge, detritus from long ago slides. They could see sheep in pastures.

Barry and Marian turned into a cutaway and sat silently soaking in the hills. Suddenly, Barry spoke calmly.

"Please tell me about your husband." Paul had been a fact, an event, a precursor to whatever this was, but he had not been brought to life before this kind Irishman.

Marian was silent, reaching within herself for the best words.

"Well, you'd like him. He was funny, kind, very reliable. People came to him in the worst days of their lives and he always helped. They wanted all of him, right away. He kept confidences well. And when other troubles appeared for clients, they

turned to him again. They could be so demanding.
So, he treasured his own private time and looked
surprised if I tried to get him back out.

Barry thought this over. "So that explains his
link in Madera."

Marian looked directly into those blue eyes.
"Barry, I know this. I love you and I will give you as
much as I can. Forever? Always? I don't know
that."

Barry leaned over to kiss her. "Marian, you may
not know, but I do. I love you fiercely and so will
my mother up in Iona. W'll go see her soon. Now if
you'll excuse me, I have to shed a tear for Ireland."
He hopped out to nearby bushes and returned
quickly. Finally, Barry started up the engine again
and slowly drove down the remaining roads to tiny
Kinvarra.

There, tucked right up to the sea's edge sat his
aunt's cottage.

"She's a sweet cushna, "Marian said softly. "Let's
go in."

Almost like fairies invading an abandoned nest,
they worked the key into the lock and opened the
door. It was all one room with a fireplace to the
right, soft chairs with wool wraps on their arms, a
small table and two chairs in a breakfast cozy

looking out onto the lawn falling down to the beach. Marian heard birds crying and then the laps of the sea, slapping the sand.

Off the central room was a door to the one bedroom and bath. That was it.

"I'll take it, breathed Marian". "This is home. Barry, I'm home."

Tears fell from both of them, tears they wiped away between long, sweet kisses.

Looking around him through Marian's eyes, Barry surrendered this special house to this woman.

"You can do anything you like to it. Anything. Just promise me you'll stay here with me."

"I will."

That was as close to a wedding as they were to get for a long time, but the cottage vow held them in each others' arms and that was all that mattered for then. Now named Cushna Cottage, the prim little house did indeed look like a "small girl."

38 Evan Smith

The following week Barry reluctantly went back to his graduate seminar at Trinity, leaving Marian at her flat on Dorset Street. Left to her own devices, she found herself in Phoenix Park wandering through the sad old Dublin Zoo. Seeing the animals frozen in concrete, padding around bare and unfriendly cages and pens, she yearned for the lushness of Costa Rica and wondered how Cara was doing with her dance project. And then Norah came to mind. Time to check in there. She phoned her immediately and got a breathless cousin on the line.

"Hey. I just ran in from the barn. So much is going on here. I don't have time to tell you everything right now but I do miss you."

"Can you get to the city for a girls' weekend?"

"Oh God, yes, that would be wonderful. Things are at a pause in construction, so…"

"Construction? What are you up to?"

Norah laughed. "God, you wouldn't believe it all. See you Friday."

Building? That sounded pretty permanent. What could it all mean? Marian crossed the Liffey at Four Courts and after trying to shop along Grafton Street with no luck, pushed her walking all the way to Trinity, and collapsed in the main library. A strong cuppa from the cafeteria anchored with a berry scone set her up for the afternoon.

As always, the Book of Kells drew her in. This incredible Bible, illustrated by the monks of Iona in the ninth century, demanded slow consideration. Each initial letter must have taken weeks to complete. Some earnest monk, one who had worked his way up in the scriptorium to the best seat, one by the window, had finally been entrusted with the shell gold. Tiny balls of pure gold, with water added to them to dissolve in the thick golden liquid to be pressed over the waiting gesso layers. He let the gold rest in a shell he scooped from the beach and cleaned just for this purpose. Each layer had dried for hours, maybe overnight, and only his breath could bring the medium to life, alive and alert enough to snatch the gold he gently lay down on it. The painted letters and text preceded the gold. The gold came last. Anything else could be ripped up, a new sheet of vellum stretched, cleaned, lined. But the gold…that was most precious and laid down on gum ammoniac, embossed with a pure agate burnisher so it would catch the glint of sun or candle and magnify the Lord.

Marian could see traces of graphite lines still there, strung from pinhole to pinhole across the manuscript. All was tightly planned, ink ground to perfect thickness, quills sharpened with a clean straight nib to move firmly down each letter, moving up to the next letter waiting for its first downward stroke. If he lifted his pen and moved to the awaiting flourish or curve, the letter waited for his touch and strokes wed seamlessly. That was joy—when the ink, vellum, and strokes all came to life. He was very good at his art. Careful not to become too proud, too sure, he prayed as he worked quickly and scraped the tiniest of rough edges away with his sharpest knife. Tiny spatters of ink were soaked up with his breakfast roll and scraped off with its hard crust. Any more work would be a sin, be excess, so he stopped and looked over every part of the page—letters, initial letter, winding illustrations of flowers and creatures looking out from the wondrous circles.

This, Marian mused, was the scribe's story. The Celtic circles amazed her for they wove in and out without error. On this page there were two sequences, painted to mirror each other in perfect harmony. Reds, blues, greens, paler shades to create illusions of shadows, all worked their paths confidently. She saw no mistakes.

Suddenly, she realized how much fun she was having. She did not have to think about how to incorporate this into her next Irish art lectures. She could just let the circle take her in, coaxing her to ignore provenance, ink and paint composition, its relation to the prior and next century. She could just look and smile.

Marian bought a hefty book in the gift shop, thinking ahead to a project she was finally acknowledging. Her time was now, not when she was aged and retired. Now. She wanted to paint, to make beautiful things from her paintings and revel in their beauty before she let them go. And she would let them all go, not hoard them with a private collector's eye.

Friday broke over Dublin with lashing rain and wind. The Liffey churned on itself, birds tucked into eaves to ride out the storm and Dubliners hunched into their coats, struggling to keep umbrellas up.

Norah tumbled into the downstairs hallway at Marian's flat and buzzed up.

"Let me in! I'm a drowned rat in your hall!"

Minutes later she shook off the rain like a wet dog and laughing, hugged Marian.

"God, you look wonderful!" Marian told her cousin. Norah's ruddy cheeks and bright eyes bore this out as true.

"Tea. A large pot, please, and I have gobs to tell you."

"It's on the boil. Tell all!"

"Gosh, where to start. Well, when you left I had many long days of waiting, wondering how much to talk to Moira about, not go too fast, you know. She was good as gold and we found our way together. We decided I am Norah Ann Malone Brach! I'd help on the farm, barn, kitchen, whatever, until about 11:00 each morning and then I'd go to Moira for lunch.

Gradually we caught up on our stories and little by little she told me much more about the Laundry days. It was worse than you can imagine. When she got out, she started a journal that went into copybooks, just pouring out of her. It's rough reading, I'll tell you that. I brought one of them for you to see, but I can't read it all with you. You'll see."

Marian poured the teas and each plunked in cream and sugar.

"Go on."

"OK, so I started to look around and take short drives around just to see what was what and have some time to myself. I had to decide where to go next. I think everyone there knew what was on my mind.

Then I took a mid-week trip on my own and spent three nights in a bed and breakfast in Carrickmacross. I loved it there. The owner was kind and not too nosey, just let me walk and see the small lake nearby and come in with my key when I liked. Breakfast was ready every morning and she waited in the kitchen for me to eat each part, poking her head in to ask would I want more tea, was I ready for eggs. I was the only one there until the last day when a family arrived for the weekend. They had stayed there often, they said, and it always felt like coming home to be there.

That was the word. Home. It did feel that way and I started thinking about Shelter Island and how I always wanted a B & B. One very windy day, Kathleen Barry, the owner, was out hanging sheets to dry. I stepped out for a chat and lent her a hand.

'It's a double clip day, that's for sure!' She laughed. I asked Kathleen what she thought about my B&B idea and she started to cry.

'I've been praying about what to do. My daughter is that sick in America and I need to go help her with the children, but I have no money. I've been sick over it, I can tell you.'

"So she agreed to sell it to me!!"
"No way."
"Way. Marian, you have to come see it and stay with me. But not yet."

"No?"
"It is a sweet place but it needs work. So Sean, the guy on the farm set me up with a friend of his who contracts out for renovations. His name is Evan Smith. Isn't that a great name?"
"Beautiful. Go on."

"So, Evan and I came up with a plan to restore the cottage to 'comfortable Irish Country.' That's what I call it, anyway. Rose Inn. Beamed ceilings, doors opening out to lawn, nooks for reading, a small turret room with an outdoor widow's walk, oh and comfy chairs, books in cases and on tables. Not fussy and ruffley. Simple, great quality and room for people to do what I did—rest, move around alone or with visitors. Good linens and old silver. A real country...home!"

"All the time?" Marian frowned, trying to imagine the drudgery ahead.

"No, no, that's the great part! I am working on themed weekends. Mystery, gourmet cooking, wine lovers, although Evan laughed at that one since Irish wine is a non- starter, but we can taste wines from all over Europe, and..."

"Whoa, sister, whoa. This sounds pretty perfect. But, back to this Evan..."

"I'm in love, Marian. Goofy in love."

"Yeah, that much I see. Is this too fast?" But Marian knew the coming answer to this one.

"You know, it's not. My whole life has been tempered, rational, slooow. This is my time and he is my guy. I know this in my bones."

The two women held each other and looked into each other's eyes.

"You won't believe what I am going to tell you, "started Marian, "but..."

"Oh God! You've found someone, too?"

And so, as rain fell, beating on the slate rood, Marian began her story about her Barry.

All the telling took time.

Soon, the two absent men seemed to be in the room with them like familiar friends.

39 Christmas 2009

Cushna House Christmas Eve

While Marian bustled bout Cushna House with greens for the mantle, paper ornaments for the small tree, all white, filling every vase and container with paperwhite flowers brought down from Dublin the day before, Barry just followed her around, smiling.

"You keep smiling like an idjit, you." Marian tossed this off with a brief kiss.

"It is all great. Brilliant, " Barry recollected. "Never had a Christmas like this. Ours were spent with nearby aunts and after dinner, paper hats and Christmas crackers. Then the adults had a few drinks, took naps, and finally, home. Not many of us, so it was not much fun, but I know they tried."

Marian looked out the kitchen window at the snow- covered grass and bushes and remembered her own Christmas past.

"I always wished for sisters and brothers, but it was just me. Mom and Dad really loved Christmas, though, and we sometimes took trips to a mountain cabin in Vermont with snow and sleds, and sometimes we'd be included in great big Christmas parties at other people's homes where I could play with other kids. I liked it.

But not as much as this year, with you. And a wedding for Norah and Evan! I can't believe it is all happening. It seems fast, but in another way, it's been years and years coming."

"Why isn't it our wedding? You know I love you and want to be with you forever." Barry's voice lowered and was intense.

"I don't know enough about myself, even yet, Barry. I love you, too.

This time, if we marry, I want a different kind of marriage and I am working on what that would look like."

"Look over here. This is what it would look like. I can wait."

And Barry crushed her into a strong hug.

"Right. Now, you go to town and check on the food deliveries and see what else I have forgotten. Chat up the baker and remind him again that the cake must be here by noon. Go!"

Barry left, full of purpose.

The phone ran and Marian heard Norah's happy voice.

"We're just off now. I have everything I can think of crammed into suitcases and bags. Evan's aunt and uncle are coming after all, so that's good. His folk are all in a dither. Moira and the farm clan are coming, of course. There will be 20 in all—is that still all right?"

"Couldn't be righter. It will be a squeeze, but so much fun. Thank God for our rebel priest. Father McHugh is coming in tomorrow. We'll be a chapel one minute and a party the next."

Norah cleared her throat and whispered with a catch in her voice, "You know I love you. This whole life would never have opened up without you. Evan and I are so grateful."

"I love you, too. It is the happiest day I can imagine. Hurry on and drive safely. See you tonight."

In the silence of the afternoon, Marian talked aloud to herself.

I am on an island and very close to living with a man I love. Last Christmas, I was on an island, too, on Shelter Island, but with no view to the future at all.

I must breathe and pray and think as I go
ahead now.
Really, I have grown up this year.
I know I am strong, can face the blackest
night.
I no longer scurry like Costa Rican ants.
  It is time to be.
God needs to enter my soul again and I need
  help in inviting this Divine in.
Barry and I will go to visit his mother on Iona
  this summer and I think she may
  be the key to the thinness of time and light
  that opens a new life. I have Paul's
  ashes with me and will scatter them in
  Ireland.
I will pack lightly for the journey.

40 Sláinte

Finally, the moment arrived.

Greens, white flowers, holly bursting with red berries covered the narrow mantel and all the tables in Cushna House. The kitchen and mudroom were transformed into a reception hall where the food lay waiting. The cake did indeed arrive on time and the rich pound cake covered in buttercream frosting with red roses all around, presided with quiet dignity on its own small table.

Evan's friend Padraic played an Irish ballad on his violin and promised jigs to follow.   And Norah entered the living room in a long, elegant white silk gown, holding her mother's hand.

Moira beamed, her smile without reserve or doubt.

She walked to Evan, also smiling from his heart, as he stood by the fireplace and placed her daughter's hand in his.

"This is a day I never believed would come. I have my girl back and with all my heart, I give her to you. Just love her."

And Moira stepped back to stand by Marian.

The priest read from the Celtic *Carmina Gadelica*.

Deep peace of the running wave to you

Deep peace of the flowing air to you

Deep peace of the quiet earth to you

Deep peace of the sleeping stones to you

Deep peace of the flock of stars to you

Prayers were said, vows made, kisses exchanged and suddenly the world was new and fine again.

Barry pronounced the final blessing:
Health and long life to you

The woman of your choice to you

A child every year to you

And may you die in Ireland.

Slainte!

It did not seem it could get any brighter, but it did.

Coming in the unlocked door, stamping snow off her boots, Cara walked into the arms of her family. Happy shouts greeted her and introductions flew around her.

"You are a gift to us. You know that, don't you?" This said through Marian's tears.

It was well past midnight before Marian and Cara collapsed in chairs before the fire.

The guests were gone; Norah and Evan off to a Paris honeymoon, and the two women sipped Irish whiskey and reflected on the year just gone.

A log crumbled and set off a gash of sparks as Marian spoke softly.

"Seeing you walk in that door today was a great moment. It really felt like we were a complete family then. You sealed it. Tell me how you managed it."

"The company decided very last minute to fill a week with concerts in London. The Cunningham Dancers had to cancel leaving a gap we could fill, so we threw our simplest sets and costumes into the trunks and took off.

It was too close and too much fun to miss this, so I decided a surprise was perfect. And I wanted to tell you in person...I have met someone. Her name is Jeanne Marie."

Glasses clinked, the fire blazed on and Marian heard all about Jeanne Marie, feeling a puzzle piece fall into place.

She would send for Nelly, stay in Ireland with Barry, meet his mother in Iona and see what happened next.

Norah would be in her Rose Inn with her Evan.

Cara was ready, as they all were, to dance.

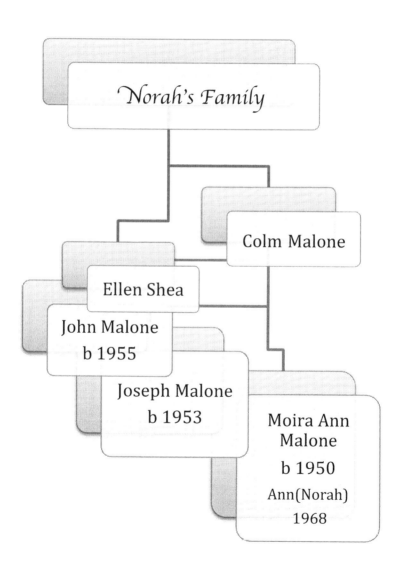

Norah's Family

Colm Malone

Ellen Shea

John Malone
b 1955

Joseph Malone
b 1953

Moira Ann
Malone
b 1950
Ann(Norah)
1968

The Three Graces: Their Family

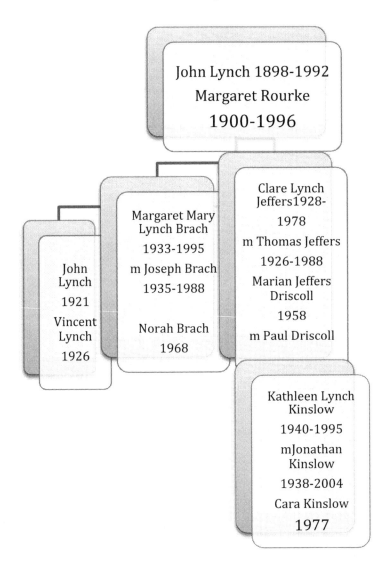

John Lynch 1898-1992
Margaret Rourke
1900-1996

John
Lynch
1921
Vincent
Lynch
1926

Margaret Mary
Lynch Brach
1933-1995
m Joseph Brach
1935-1988

Norah Brach
1968

Clare Lynch
Jeffers1928-
1978
m Thomas Jeffers
1926-1988
Marian Jeffers
Driscoll
1958
m Paul Driscoll

Kathleen Lynch
Kinslow
1940-1995
mJonathan
Kinslow
1938-2004
Cara Kinslow
1977

About the author

Nan Deane Cano is the author of **Acts of Light: Martha Graham in the 21st Century**, University Press Florida, photograhy by John Deane. She is an adjunct faculty member of California Lutheran University in the Graduate School of Education. Her work has appeared in numerous magazines, **The New York Times** and the **Los Angeles Times**. She is also a member of the Immaculate Heart Community.

Acknowledgements

Absorbing as it does the years of my life,
The Three Graces owes its bones to my Irish
immigrant family. My writing group adventures in
Costa Rica with Writer Laureate of Alaska, Peggy
Schumacher and Los Angeles Poet Laureate Eloise
Klein Healy nurtured the prose over several years.
Helen Anne Mack generously offered personal
reminiscences of Irish adoption. My husband
Thomas became the model muse. There could be no
substitute for the careful eye of my copy editor,
Kathleen Cole. Many thanks to my brother John
Deane for his faithful reading and support and to
treasured Nobue Hirabayashi at Mt.Design for
cover and art direction. The Martha Graham Dance
Company once again opened their creative doors to
me for this novel. Particular thanks to Artistic
Director Janet Eilber, Principal Dancers Miki
Orihara,Elizabeth Auclair, Heidi Stoeckley (retired)
and Director Virginie Mecene. Interviews with
Erica Dankmeyer deepened my understanding of
the process in creating an original dance. My

Immaculate Heart Community lives and breathes what a vital religious community can do in today's world and stands in happy contrast to the dearth of spiritual life the cousins found in this novel. Immaculate Heart College, a bastion of clear and creative thinking for 65 years,closed in 1981. I have brought this wonderful institution back to life and placed her near the Pacific Ocean.

Sadly, the Magdalene Laundries were not fiction. They existed throughout Ireland until 1996. Indeed, more Magdalene Laundries were scattered throughout Europe, Canada and the United States. Over 30,000 women served as inmates over time, including the singer Sinead O'Connor. The plight of those inmates is chronicled in the film *The Magdalenes* directed by Peter Mullan. Further information regarding this blight on Ireland can be found online at *Justice for Magdalenes*. Helpful print resources are *Banished Babies* by Mike Milotte and *Do Penance or Perish* by Frances Finnegan.

On February 19,2013, Irish Prime Minister Enda Kenny issued a full state apology to the women of the Magdalene Laundries. He described the laundries as "the nation's disgrace."

Made in the USA
San Bernardino, CA
21 April 2018